## What the critics are saying…

*5 STARS* "The sex between Serosen and Selena is hot enough to singe the fingertips, and in fact, nearly melted my computer screen…" ~ *Reva Moore Just Erotic Romance Newsletter*

"*Ms. Donovan* draws in her readers and sweeps us away. The danger and the suspense in this story are riveting. I was on the edge of my seat through all of it…Passion, magick, love, danger, strong characters, a sexy as sin hero and a spitfire heroine can be found within the pages of *Wicked Pleasure* that *Ms. Donovan* writes magnificently." ~ *Tracey West The Road to Romance*

"*Ms. Donovan* writes a fabulously intricate tale that brings you into her world and makes you want to stay." ~ *Cathleen Cody Romance Junkies*

"This well-written story from Ellora's Cave is another winning romantica offering. The spicy hot sex is the perfect punctuation for the fast-paced fantasy plot." ~ *April Chase Romance Studio*

*5 ROSES* "*Wicked Pleasures* was a great, erotic, fantasy romance read; it contained action, great characters, and fantastic world-building." *Marelee Breakfield Escape to Romance*

# Nelissa Donovan

Ellora's Cave
Romantica Publishing

An Ellora's Cave Romantica Publication

www.ellorascave.com

Night Elves: Wicked Pleasures

ISBN # 1419950576
ALL RIGHTS RESERVED.
Wicked Pleasures Copyright© 2003 Nelissa Donovan
Edited by: Ann Richardson
Cover art by: Darrell King

Electronic book Publication: November, 2003
Trade paperback Publication: October, 2005

With the exception of quotes used in reviews, this book may not be reproduced or used in whole or in part by any means existing without written permission from the publisher, Ellora's Cave Publishing, Inc.® 1056 Home Avenue, Akron OH 44310-3502.

This book is a work of fiction and any resemblance to persons, living or dead, or places, events or locales is purely coincidental. The characters are productions of the authors' imagination and used fictitiously.

# Warning:

The following material contains graphic sexual content meant for mature readers. *Night Elves: Wicked Pleasures* has been rated *E-rotic* by a minimum of three independent reviewers.

Ellora's Cave Publishing offers three levels of Romantica™ reading entertainment: S (S-ensuous), E (E-rotic), and X (X-treme).

S-en*suous* love scenes are explicit and leave nothing to the imagination.

E-*rotic* love scenes are explicit, leave nothing to the imagination, and are high in volume per the overall word count. In addition, some E-rated titles might contain fantasy material that some readers find objectionable, such as bondage, submission, same sex encounters, forced seductions, etc. E-rated titles are the most graphic titles we carry; it is common, for instance, for an author to use words such as "fucking", "cock", "pussy", etc., within their work of literature.

X-*treme* titles differ from E-rated titles only in plot premise and storyline execution. Unlike E-rated titles, stories designated with the letter X tend to contain controversial subject matter not for the faint of heart.

Also by Nelissa Donovan:

Night Elves: Dangerous Obsession
Hearts are Wild *(Anthology)*

# Wicked Pleasures
*Night Elves*

# Chapter One

*The fires burn so fiercely. It's as if their unholy souls work to wreak some last revenge before melting into the abyss.*

Serosen pushed a shining strand of midnight hair behind his gracefully arched ear and signaled to his bowman.

"Let us be away, Vigil. Our work here is done."

A shadowy form wavered then disengaged from the ancient oak, solidifying into an agile, heavily muscled youth. The pattern on his skin, like Serosen's, twined with dark blue spirals and symbols from wrist to arm, disappearing beneath the charcoal tunic, to emerge at the neck and up one side of his angular face.

Vigil lowered his intricately carved bow and nodded. *"Yes, brother."*

Only those privy to Tuathan elf-speak could hear the silent exchange, but even among the People, the talent was becoming scarce. As Serosen breathed in the deep green scents of the *P'car* forest, every muscle on his lean, cat-like form filled with the sizzling energy of the woodland and its magickal denizens. At the outskirts of the Winter Kingdome, *P'car* brimmed with life—quite unlike the frozen heart at the center of the intimidating demesne.

Once fortified with the sustaining elements of air, earth and wind, the pair slipped through the forest at lightning speed in a variegated blur against the night time hues of blue, gray and verdant green.

Serosen needed little concentration to manage his pace and direction, and his thoughts wandered. *So much killing. So many of our mothers and sisters lost.*

Things had gone from bad to worse for the People. Summer, Spring, Autumn Kingdome—it mattered not from which tribe the Tuatha hailed, each had been subject to equally vicious raids by the Unsellie Court, led by their brutal emperor, Garethan. And since the underworld scum had fortified their ranks with the magickally created Golem legion, it was becoming more difficult for the Tuathan warriors to protect their borders, and more importantly, their women.

Nigh impossible—in some places.

As he ran, an image crashed into Serosen's mind. A long row of chained Tuathan women, naked, beautiful and shining even in their bonded state, being herded like human cattle through underground vaults of brimstone and flint. Leering Golems—filthy, disproportionate beings of earth and vileness—prodded the women along. The Golems' limb-like manhoods bulging, their black-fingered hands pinching their captives' cream-pale nipples and—

Liquid fire erupted through Serosen's veins, and it was only Vigil's warning mind-touch that prevented him from unleashing a sizzling bolt of elf-fire at the nearest tree.

*"You will stop them, brother. It is only through you that we have been able to safeguard our Kingdome's borders from Garethan's raids."*

*"Kindly refrain from partaking of my personal thoughts, elfling,"* Serosen grumbled, annoyed that his emotions had made loose with his thoughts and powers, and that it took a touch from his younger brother to remind him to rein in his control.

Vigil flashed him an intense gaze the color of polished golden oak, as they surged through tree and rock. *He looks so much like our mother, Goddess rest her soul,* thought Serosen, as a fresh stab of loss filled his heart.

*"I speak only the truth. You always know where the Golems seek to raid. There is no denying that your vision and destructive art are great."*

Serosen swallowed a denunciation. Night Elves were known for their candor and brutal sense of honesty, unlike many of their Tuathan cousins who would speak any flowery lie that served their whim or plotting design.

Vigil was right. At nearly five-hundred years old, Serosen was just coming into his prime, yet his gifts had grown and expanded as if he were crossing the path into Timelessness, instead of youthful middle age. Even the Elders had consulted on his unusual abilities, yet mysteriously refrained from sharing their conclusions about his extraordinary talents with the tribe.

Not that Serosen was complaining. For a Night Ranger, the power of sight was all-important, as was the honed skill of stalking and dispatching enemy or prey, whether with a heart-seeking arrow or a mind-attack like elf-fire.

As they continued to shimmer their way around and through elm and ash, Serosen harkened back to the Dark Years. Night Rangers were known as Nightmare Destroyers then, for their consummate skill of eliminating their foes en-route. Through mind-travel, they could "see" the intentions of their enemy before they arrived, and be waiting—to destroy.

Serosen needed no army to take care of business. With a trusted bowman at his side to guard him should he need to mind-travel, Serosen could incinerate a small army without great risk to himself.

Or regret.

A sudden shock to the land beneath their flying feet brought Serosen and Vigil to a head-snapping halt.

Vigil gripped an ancient ash to steady himself. "What ails the land, Ser?" he said aloud, elf-speak and formalities falling away in light of the jarring concussion.

His body taut, Serosen crouched. He gripped the black soil. "Guard, Vigil."

Without another word, Vigil freed his bow and melted into the forest.

And in an instant, Serosen detached from his flesh and was away. His mind's eye zagged through earth, tree and rock, searching for the source of the disturbance. Some being had trespassed on sacred *Tir na n-Og* land.

He came to an immediate halt in the Summer Kingdome, where the sun shone more hours than any other demesne, home of his licentious cousin, Prince Du'an.

And there he found the impeccably tall, golden-haired, green-eyed Du'an, pushing a petite, auburn-haired beauty to the lush meadow floor. His hands made short work of her clinging shirt, revealing golden-skinned breasts straining to overflow their lacy bonds.

*Nothing new about this scene.* So why had his mind-travel brought him to witness his cousin coupling with a jean-clad Terran—

TERRAN.

Serosen's vision-self shuddered with shock and fury. *This is forbidden!*

For over two-hundred years it had been strictly prohibited for any Tuathan to activate a portal to their sister world. Not for *any* reason, let alone one as simple as luring an attractive female into a lustful encounter. Since the Unsellie Court had brokered rogue mages to scan for gateway activity, it was deemed too risky to put their naïve and powerless sister world at risk. At least the Tuatha had the means to fight and repel the Unsellie scum. Earth had no resources to protect against the magickal race and keep the Unsellie from stealing the Terran women and children to use as breeders and slaves.

A low moan brought Serosen's attention back to the couple. Du'an had the Terran completely disrobed now, and he gently laid her upon the jasmine-scented grass. Her head was tipped up, her lips parted as she gave another throaty groan. Serosen's spirit-gaze traveled down her slender neck to her fully exposed, delicious breasts. His steel-gray eyes fastened on the maiden's coin-sized, burgundy nipples, and Serosen could swear the throbbing buds stiffened under his stare.

His loins ached with an intense longing. With the threat to the Tuatha, the Night Elves' women had been sequestered in a well-guarded place, rendering the act of lovemaking something one had to plan in detail to execute. Not that someone of Serosen's position would have trouble finding a willing bedmate even in seclusion, but truth be told, there were few he *hadn't* found pleasure with already. And Serosen's taste of the oftentimes wicked mind games many of them played had curbed his appetite as of late.

Serosen was certain his physical manhood back in the forested glade was stiff with desire, and he could only imagine what Vigil was thinking. Probably wishing he could mind-link with his brother to get a taste of what he was missing, but Vigil wasn't advanced enough to attempt such a thing—or so Vigil's teachers had led Serosen to believe. He wasn't at all convinced that his younger brother wasn't hiding much of his gifts from the *Arrowen* masters. With that in mind, Serosen blocked his thoughts to all possible interference and moved in closer.

The magick-drugged Terran eased her legs apart and drew pink-tipped fingers lazily up one inner thigh to the tapered thatch of reddish curls. Serosen longed to be the one between the lustful Terran's thighs as she began to lightly tease the glistening, rosy nub with her index finger. Serosen barely held back a moan as the musky scent of the woman's liquid desire filled his senses.

"Oh, yes, sweetling. Envision my cock inside of you…thrusting, filling you," murmured Du'an.

Serosen's spirit-gaze flicked to his cousin's now naked and glowing back. If he wished it, he could easily infiltrate Du'an's mind to experience the beguiling maiden's pulsating warmth in the flesh. But no, it wouldn't truly be *his* flesh entering the maiden's fiery cave, or *his* ethereal seed spilling deep into her womb.

*Enough!*

Serosen tried to shake himself free of the lust-induced haze that worked to control his judgment. Du'an's thoughtless act had exposed his Kingdome and the maiden's world to unspeakable danger.

Serosen knew that Du'an preferred to build desire and expectations to a fever pitch before actually coupling with his mate, and it would leave them unsuspecting targets for the Golems. Serosen could already feel the filthy wretches breeching the Summer demesne in their haste to reach the duo and the contact point for the portal.

With one last hungry look at the luscious Terran, Serosen flung his will to the wind and rode it back to his body in the *P'car* Forest. He slammed into his physical form and stood. Energy sizzled along his nerves and exited in sparkles of ice-blue light through the ancient markings that spiraled the left side of his lithe form.

He was instantly aware of his painfully hot erection straining against his deerskin breeches. No time to relieve his need. Being consummate master of his body, Serosen calmed the blood surging through his cock before calling for Vigil.

His bowman slipped down from the twining rowan tree above Serosen's head, his amber, almond-shaped eyes ripe with amusement.

Serosen scanned the clearing, searching for the entrance to the sacred path. "I must leave you and take the sacred path to the Summer Kingdome."

Vigil grabbed Serosen's arm, turning his brother to face him. "Ser, you know you are not allowed to use the path—"

"Enough!" Serosen shook Vigil's hand away.

His brother's ebony and chestnut streaked hair bristled with irritation, and Serosen felt a pang of regret at his harshness.

He stepped in close and placed a hand on Vigil's shoulder. "You must trust me. Travel as swiftly as possible to Whitecliff and warn the Elder Council that the Caledonian portal in the Summer Kingdome has been breeched."

With that he knelt, taking a pinch of Winter Kingdome earth and placing it in the leather pouch at his waist. He stood and breathed deeply, drawing in all the forest had to offer. He would need the borrowed energy for what lay ahead.

"Ser," Vigil started, his voice deep with concern.

Serosen leveled a somber look at his brother. "The Golems are on their way to intercept the gatekeeper. I intend to stop them, but there is only one way for me to arrive in time."

Vigil's golden eyes narrowed and his finely-chiseled nostrils flared. He inclined his head. "May your travel be as swift as the wind that guides you."

Serosen stood and the tribe-mates clasped arms, their markings lancing a brilliant blue where they touched.

"For *Tir na n-Og*, brother," said Vigil.

"*For* Tir na n-Og," Serosen responded in elf-speak.

## Chapter Two

*Glowing…his skin…like morning sunshine…hot, so hot! And his fingers, long, smooth, but he isn't touching… No, it's my fingers, stroking. Oh my God…*

Selena moaned, delicious pleasure building, until she felt certain she would explode. Her senses were on fire, touch, smell, taste, *sight.*

*What's happening?* Selena's questions were thrust aside by electric, sensual sensations that occupied every inch of space.

"Such an exquisite specimen of mortal flesh," came a deep, resonate voice.

The sound vibrated through her entire being, drawing even more liquid warmth to coat her now thrusting fingers.

"Yes, my sweetling…that's it. Drive those fine, precious fingers deeper. Teasing… ah, yes."

Selena complied without question, the tips of her fingers flicking against her clit with an almost desperate rhythm.

*So swollen…so close, so near!* But there was something holding her back…something keeping her on the precipice, dangling, without release as the fire continued to build—and burn.

"Open your eyes, woman." His voice went from sexy to severe in an instant.

She did, her eyes taking in the full measure of him. He loomed above her. His golden-white hair swirled and flowed around well-muscled shoulders as if it had a life of its own. And his eyes, deep verdant pools pinned Selena to the earth at her back with an almost physical pressure. Her gaze lowered, past the flat, rippling muscles of his abdomen, to the light dusting of flaxen hair…

Selena gasped. Even through the passion-haze, the shock of seeing the stranger's massive, throbbing member above her prone body threw her into confusion.

"Where am I? What's going—?"

The creature knelt and placed a warm finger on her parted lips. "Shhhh…"

His touch arced through her, making her lips and tongue tingle. Selena could feel his rigid staff pressing against her belly, and a staggering image of the golden god coming at her from behind filled her mind. She groaned, fear and confusion bleeding away, leaving nothing but an all-consuming desire.

"Yes," Selena whispered, her voice sounding strange and lilting to her ears. She spread her legs wider and thrust her hips upward. "Fill me. Let me have all of you."

He chuckled and traced a finger down her chin to her throat, leaving a burning trail. "Not yet, my brave little maiden. We have forever to play, you and I. And the playing is the best part."

Selena shook her head. "No, no…I-I…"

Her words died in her throat as his head dipped and his lips fastened on her nipple, drawing it in against teeth and tongue, suckling, pulling the entire areola into the hot recesses of his mouth. She bucked against his hard body and cried out for a release that wouldn't come. All of

Selena's muscles contracted as he continued to flick and tease the swollen bud. Her fingers worked harder within her shuddering wetness, searching, begging for climax.

"Oh God," Selena moaned, "what are you doing to me?"

His muted laughter filled her head as he moved from one aching nipple to the other.

*"Loving you, sweetling...loving you as only a Tuathan Summer Prince can."*

"An asinine Summer Prince with curdled cheese for brains," came a husky, irate male voice.

Selena cried out as the golden god's mouth left her throbbing nipples. She tried to turn her head to see who the intrusive voice belonged to, but found she could not. She could only stare at the naked, flaxen-haired creature poised above her, his grass-green eyes focused on the intruder. His lip curled as he spoke. "*Cousin.* Couldn't you have arranged a more seemly time to visit? Surely you can see that I am occupied."

"Which is the very reason I am here, *cousin,*" replied the dark and sultry voice. "You know what you have done is forbidden, *dangerous.*"

Another laugh rumbled through her delicious tormentor's chest. "*Life* is dangerous, Serosen, or haven't you noticed?"

*Serosen.* The name vibrated through Selena's psyche, sending an odd, disconcerting tingle up her spine.

Again, a small, reasoning edge teased at the corners of her mind.

*Where am I?*

Footsteps brought the intruder closer. A musky aroma of night blooming nicotiana and honeyed spice filled Selena's senses. Bringing with it more awareness, more questions.

*What in the hell am I doing here? Where is here? And who is the naked guy on top of me?*

"Release the maiden and leave. Even now they are coming for you. If you hadn't been otherwise occupied, you might have felt them."

Selena's gaze was still fixated on the ethereal creature above her, but her senses were reaching for the voice—for the tinge of awareness his presence wrought. The golden god's expression flickered a moment of panic, then his eyes narrowed with fury.

"'Tis not possible! Cresen swore the charm would shield my passage."

"Then Cresen is a fool. And you are ten times a centaur's ass for believing him, Du'an. Now go!"

Du'an stood to his full height, leaving Selena cold in the absence of his wonderful warmth. The golden god snarled. "Do not presume to order me, cousin."

A sigh, and suddenly there was a twisted dagger at Du'an's throat. Selena's gaze brushed the intruder's hand. It was dusky-skinned, the wrist and forearm rippling with muscle as it held the wicked ebony blade dead still against the golden god's convulsing Adam's apple.

"We do not have time for your petty attitude or games. Do not doubt that I will spill your life force before allowing the Unsellie to use you to access the gate."

Selena could feel the bonds of passion loosening. Not enough to provide release to the urgent, throbbing need, but enough for her muddled brain to realize she was completely outside her own reality — and that the creatures above her represented a volatile, unknown danger.

And yet...she wanted *him* still. Deep inside her. Riding her with deep, penetrating strokes.

\* \* \* \* \*

The maiden moaned, and Serosen could feel Du'an reasserting his pull on the Terran's passion-drugged mind. He leaned in, pressing the tip of the obsidian dagger into the flesh of Du'an's throat. "Release her, troll spawn. What care you for this wicked pleasure when your father's Kingdome is about to be compromised? Have you no loyalty?"

Du'an threw back his head and laughed. "What will be left to inherit, Serosen? My *Kingdome* has been nearly raped dry. My mother and aunt — gone. My sisters in hiding." He lowered his liquid eyes to the maiden and sneered. With an almost unnoticeable wave of his left hand, he caused the Terran to arch her back and gasp, her burgundy nipples puckering. Serosen felt a tightening in his groin at the sight, and fought the urge to run his hand over her delectable mounds.

As if reading his thoughts, Du'an moved around the dagger, leaned down and flicked one of the rosy buds, sending the maiden into mews of delight. "What is there left to do but find pleasure? To indulge as we were meant to? Instead we allow Garethan and his Unsellie scum to manipulate our lives." He pointed to his chest. "*Us*, Serosen. The most superior and honored of all the fey, driven to hiding our women and wealth, and defending against border raids like pathetic medieval humans."

Tearing his eyes away from the maid, Serosen lowered the dagger and gathered his thoughts. He didn't have time to agree or disagree with his cousin's reasoning. The Golems were closer—their putrid bodies desecrating the forest as they pushed onward. A blaze burned in his chest at the thought of the monsters getting their hands on the harmless maid. What they would do to her…? Serosen blocked the image, fury threatening to overwhelm him.

"Enough. You must leave. Would you allow the Unsellie to gain their strongest foothold on *Tir na n-Og* in the Summer Kingdome? Think of your sisters, Du'an."

Du'an smirked, stood, and with a flick of his wrist, he was once again fully clothed. "Far be it for me to stand in the way of our darkling prince reducing the Golem minions to ash." He knelt beside the maiden, and reached out a hand. "Come, sweetling. We will take our pleasure elsewhere. Away from my death-minded cousin."

"No!" Serosen stepped in, a surge of protectiveness making him see red. "Leave her. She will be a beacon to the Unsellie and their mages. Wherever she goes, they will follow. The maiden must go back to her own world—after I've dispatched with this threat."

Du'an stood, his normally warm eyes cooling, before he broke out in laughter. He looked from the writhing maiden to Serosen and grinned. "Now I understand. You want her for yourself." He raised one finely arched brow. "Perhaps you are not as insipid as you look, cousin."

A palpable stench wafted into the clearing, and Serosen crouched. "They come. Go, Du'an, *now!*"

Serosen watched his cousin's face pale, before he gave an impish grin. "Consider her your recompense, Serosen—if you survive."

Du'an whistled for his silver steed. The elfin stallion materialized from the woods at its master's side, its black eyes rolling wildly at the Golem reek. Du'an mounted and was away in a frenzied blur.

Serosen let out an annoyed breath and knelt at the maiden's side. Her eyes were closed, her lips slightly parted as her slender finger continued to tease her swollen button.

*Centaur's balls. He's left her bewitching intact!*

He knew that Du'an was powerful enough in the erotic arts to maintain the enchantment for as long as the maid remained in *Tir na n-Og*.

Serosen's tattoos tingled…the swirling, interconnected blue patterns warning of impending threat.

No time to reach his cousin's mind and demand the maid's release.

He slipped his hand under the small of her back and lifted the auburn-haired beauty in one swift move. She gasped at the flesh-to-flesh contact, and Serosen's body jerked as a ripple of wild energy pulsed throughout his entire form.

He stared down at the Terran's now open, azure eyes, his heart thudding. *Her eyes…blue and deep as the Ta'loch pools.*

"I know you," she said, her lilting voice clear as the rushing falls that emptied into the eternal abyss. "I've known you my entire life, my dark prince."

# Chapter Three

"'Tis not possible," the dusky-skinned god whispered.

His steel-gray eyes locked with Selena's, and a shaft of clarity filled her. She reached up and brushed fingertips down the side of his noble jaw, stopping at the swirled bands of blue. "My dreams. Since I was a little girl. You were always there — watching. In the bark of the cottonwoods and palo verdes surrounding our home. You were my guardian."

His arresting face paled. "How —" His head whipped toward the dense copse of trees to their left, and Selena felt his body tense. "They come." His voice was a whisper, but the force of it shot through Selena like cathedral bells at Sunday mass. As if she were no more than a five-pound sack of flour, Selena found herself slung over broad shoulders, her head hanging above olive-clad, muscled buttocks.

A ripple of desire flushed through her anew, and Selena fought to maintain the sliver of awareness that had filled her at her dark prince's touch. *Don't let it take over again, Selena...don't —*

They were flying.

The ground beneath her was a blur of muted browns and vibrant splashes of green. *No. Not flying. We're still on the ground — barely.*

With a snapping jolt they came to a halt and Selena was flung onto a soft patch of fragrant alyssum. The sweet perfume filled her senses, an instant before a putrid reek assaulted her.

Her desire was instantly curbed as she slapped a hand over her nose and mouth. *What's that stench?*

The hard-bodied, pointy-eared creature knelt beside her, and for the first time, Selena's senses were somewhat clear—if completely confused. His eyes fastened on her, and Selena felt that tingle.

*I must be dreaming. That's it. I must have drunk myself blind at Gwen's grad party and passed out. That's why I can't wake up. That's why my dark prince is here.*

"Stay within the alyssum and hold on to this." He thrust a pouch into her hands, and as her fingers closed around it, Selena could have sworn she felt a shifting within the bag. As if it contained a living creature.

*Gross!*

A muscled hand closed around hers and squeezed. "Do not let go. If events go poorly, open it and mark your face with the contents."

Their eyes met, and Selena shivered at the intensity of his unearthly gaze. Selena longed to trace the strange tattoos that twined up the side of his noble jaw and cheek.

He broke eye contact first and stood with the grace of a panther. Selena watched her dark prince stride forward then stop. His long, midnight hair flowed around broad shoulders as if teased by invisible fingers, his body taut.

*He's glowing. Oh, my God. His entire body…shining. No, pulsating. The light—a violet blue.*

Selena shivered and clutched the bag. She felt a steady pounding in the earth, and her gaze rose as creatures broke free of the trees and into the narrow clearing.

She gasped.

*Monsters. Demons!*

The horrid creatures stopped when they saw the dark prince, and howled. Their massive jaws unhinged, showing yellow, jagged-edged teeth.

*And the stench.* It slammed into Selena like a sledgehammer, driving her further into the alyssum. Dew from the tiny white flowers cooled her backside, and with eyes watering, she looked to…*what had the golden god called him? Serosen?* His body arced with a brilliant light as he faced the monsters.

*There are so many of them.*

A voice erupted in her head. *"Close your eyes!"*

Without hesitation, Selena obeyed. Light—white and blinding filled her senses, burned through her eyelids and into the core of her being. Selena screamed, squeezing her eyes tighter. She gasped for air as an incredible pressure forced her onto her back. The very ground heaved beneath her.

Acrid smoke filled her nostrils. *Burning…everything is burning!*

She thought she heard screams—howls of fury and pain, and the crackling of a forest on fire. Her fingers dug into the cool soil, and she held on for dear life.

And then it was still.

Afraid to breathe deeply, she pressed her face into the alyssum and groaned. As the world settled around her, and the horror of the past minutes faded, Selena's burgeoning clarity began to drift away, as if on an outgoing tide.

*No! Stay aware, Selena…don't slip back into…*

\* \* \* \* \*

Serosen moved to the maid and gently pulled her up off the ground—which was now burning. The liquid white flames had yet to reach the damp green of the alyssum patch, but they soon would. His gaze flicked to the ashy lumps that littered the forest floor. Slight overkill. He hadn't meant to generate such a blast—at least not one that damaged the forest so appallingly. The little deaths of sapling and plant pierced his soul, but it was far better than the alternative, and the flames would soon be squelched by the coming rain. The forest knew how to protect its own.

At least the maid seemed unharmed. His hand nearly encircled her slender arm twice, his skin dark against her petal soft, golden-hue. Her brilliant blue eyes were half-closed, with no hint of the awareness she bore a moment before when danger threatened. She was so small. Her head only came to his shoulder, but her breasts, hips and ass were generously rounded. He ran a hand through her luxurious locks. The fire-touched threads woven amongst the auburn made her thick tresses shimmer and glisten like liquid flame.

She moaned at his touch, and as her fingers curled around his bicep, Serosen felt a quickening in his groin. *Curse Du'an.* The maid had fallen back into Du'an's enchantment now that her preservation instinct had passed. She leaned into him, and her bare, puckered nipples burned right through the cloth separating them. Serosen's cock strained against his breeches.

*Goddess, I don't have time for this.* He knew he should push her away—put distance between them as he considered his next step—but never had he felt skin so soft. Never had his eyes feasted on woman flesh so utterly delectable.

Serosen traced a finger over the back of her arm, up to the fine arch of her shoulder. He stopped at a beguiling mole, the size of a pippin seed, a perfect accompaniment to her golden skin, and he itched to lave at it with his very flexible tongue. To feel her shift and writhe beneath his artful ministrations.

*A few moments. Only a few, small moments.*

Serosen wound his other hand around the maid's slender waist, his palm coming to rest against the generous curve of her hip. She quivered beneath his touch. A small, cool hand covered Serosen's and pushed it toward the fine, narrow strip of auburn hair above her slit.

His fingers twined through the silky pelt and slipped into the maid's warm folds. Fluid ambrosia drenched his gently stroking fingers, and she pressed herself with amazing force against his cupped hand.

Serosen shifted his hand just enough to allow the maid to impale herself upon a single finger. Her channel was so tight and hot, Serosen's thoughts shifted to him burying himself in her to the hilt.

Serosen's breath caught as he fought a maddening desire to throw the woman onto the smoldering forest floor and thrust his painfully rigid staff into her luscious, dripping box.

Laughter erupted in Serosen's mind. *"Take her, cousin. Bring her to climax and you will have broken my enchantment, freeing her from such sweet torment."*

Serosen tensed and flung his cousin from his mind. There were few Tuathan who could sustain forcible contact with him 'less he allowed it. Du'an was not one of them. Serosen looked down on the auburn head of his unwitting seductress. She continued to press herself against him, her hands shifting over his arms and chest, leaving fiery trails on his skin despite the tunic between them.

He shifted slightly, and the maid groaned, rocking forward on his finger, which nearly made him spill his seed where he stood. Serosen cursed as he breathed in her intoxicating scent, fragrant sweet sage, with just a hint of citrus.

*I could take her. Break Du'an's spell, then put her back through the gate just after –*

"'Twould be a most disadvantageous decision," came a chiming voice.

Serosen's eyes riveted to the pale apparition that fluttered a hairsbreadth from his cheek.

*Ferra'leen.* Daughter of the High Queen of Faerie. Rarely seen, and even less frequently heard. The heady scent of lavender and roses flowed over him, and Serosen was quick to ward both he and the maid from the faerie's alluring perfume.

"Princess," Serosen said with a nod, careful to keep his voice low and respectful. "Your words are always wise. May I be so bold as to ask why?"

"Many may not, but for you, young prince, I would answer."

## Chapter Four

Ferra'leen flitted backward, and in an aching flash of diamond-white, she appeared before Serosen in her heightened form. The faerie folded brilliant opalescent wings to her sides as silver hair cascaded around her bare figure and twined against her slender curves.

Serosen kept his position, the Terran maid in his arms rocking hot upon his finger, his cock still rigid. He felt no shame, for in *Tir na n-Og* partaking of bodily pleasure was as natural as breathing, or magick, and often integral to both.

The princess moved closer, her eyes gazing with frank appraisal at the maid's delicious curves and passion-infused features. Serosen met Ferra'leen's depthless violet eyes, and smiled.

She returned the grin, a strand of luminescent hair flicking out to caress the girl's bare shoulder. "She is lovely. A gracious choice for our normally ungracious Du'an to make. Perhaps there is hope for him after all."

Serosen hmphed, and Ferra'leen's tinkling laughter zinged along his spine.

"Come, come…" A willowy hand went to her lips to stifle another giggle. "I beg your highness's forgiveness for such a slip of the tongue. And after I inform you what a mistake it would be to relieve yourself thusly within this amazing specimen of earthly delight."

Serosen sighed internally. Now this was more like the Ferra'leen he knew and mistrusted. Full of poorly veiled innuendo and precocious deeds. Even so, it was unusual for her to approach him unattended, what with the tension between the races as of late. The Tuatha were certain Garethan had sent representatives to try to woo the Faerie Realm to the Unsellie's ends, and yet the faerie continued to deny such to the Tuatha, which bred a powerful aura of suspicion and mistrust.

But it wouldn't pay to have Ferra'leen aware of his discomfiture.

"She is quite lovely, is she not?" Serosen bent close to the maid's graceful neck and breathed in the alluring spice of her sex. The aroma alone ignited his passion once again to a near feverish need.

*Perhaps Du'an has manipulated some charm onto me as well?* thought Serosen, fighting to control his desire.

"Such a fool for an insightful Dark Ranger. You are much too powerful and well-warded by your elders for that to occur."

Serosen forced his attention away from the Terran maid to gaze at Ferra'leen. Her angular and shining face was serious beyond measure, her crimson lips a thin line of impatience.

"I thought you brighter than that, young prince. To not have figured this out on your own is testament to the Terran's oblique influence." She raised a finely arched brow and stared at the girl with disdain—and something else. Interest, perhaps, or hunger. "Odd, but fascinating."

Serosen felt a tightening in his gut. A forewarning of peril, the abrupt sensation putting a marginal damper on his need.

Ferra'leen's petite head cocked, as if listening to an inner dialogue, which Serosen had no doubt she had done. "My time is short. So I will be direct." Silvery light began to pulsate farther from her body. Her wings burst forth, wafting faerie musk, deep and fragrant, around the trio. "Thanks to your witless cousin, this ordinary Terran is now a valuable link in stimulating a portal. Her world's pull will be on her, wanting to right what Du'an has tampered with. The maid will be a compass for Garethan and his minions, and should they lay hands on her—"

"I realize th—"

"Silence!" Ferra'leen hissed as she rose, her wings beating an ominous rhythm into the still night air. "You do not understand the full implications, princeling. If you spill your seed inside this Terran maid, she will no longer be connected to Du'an, true, but she will then be bound to you, Winter Prince."

The faerie whipped to one side of the entwined pair, silver hair writhing. "And where you go, she will be bound to go. And it will then be *you* the Golems pursue. It will be *you* Garethan will unleash his Unsellie forces against." Amethyst sparks flickered from Ferra'leen's eyes. "Why do you think Du'an is now encouraging you to take the maid? He has been informed of his deep folly, and seeks to pacify those who would berate him for endangering his demesne. If you mate with this—woman, it will be your Kingdome made vulnerable by a worthless piece of Terran flesh."

A fine chill stole through Serosen and he gently removed his finger from the maid's hot slit. She gasped, and made to push herself once more upon his hand, but as painful as it was, Serosen grabbed her upper arms and held her away from him. His entire form rebelled at the thought that he would not be able to release her—and himself—from this sweet torture.

But he understood the implications. Knew them, really, before Ferra'leen gave voice to them. Perhaps it was the passion of battle and high magick that had muddled his good sense.

His steel-gray gaze rose to meet Ferra'leen's glowing purple orbs. "I will send her directly back through the nearest Winter Gate, taking the sacred path to—"

"No!" screeched the faerie, her wings now beating the air in agitation. "There is no time, and it is forbidden to expose the sacred channel to a Terran's foul energy. You push boundaries by crossing within the path yourself!"

Serosen's eyes narrowed. Something wasn't right. Ferra'leen's original attempt at bestowing valuable information upon him was now brimming with undercurrents of malice, or perhaps it always had been, but he'd been too enraptured by the maid to notice.

Ferra'leen flew closer, her features suddenly sharp and feral in the shadows of the forest canopy despite her internal glow. She reached out a long-nailed finger. "Give her to me. I can transport her to Faerie and dispose of her there without great risk to myself or my Kingdome."

"Dispose of her?" Serosen turned the maid and pulled her in tight to his chest. "Just how would you do that, Ferra'leen? Nightshade poison or a dwarf-wrought blade?"

A piercing squeal sliced through the glade as the faerie shrunk to half her size and fluttered menacingly around Serosen's head. "Fool! She must be eliminated to prevent further contamination. Even an Ogre can see you haven't the stomach for it. Leave her to me!"

Anger, quick and fierce, suffused Serosen. "This audience is at a close, *your highness.*" Ignoring the high-pitched shrills of fury at his back, he slung the Terran over his shoulder and pulled the forest energies to him in a single breath. Power surged along his sculpted form and through his rushing veins, quelling some of his desire, but igniting another — to silence the faerie with a frightening blow of elf-fire.

*Which I cannot — must not do.*

The last thing the Tuatha needed was a war with Faerie. Not that it mightn't come to that. But he would not be the one to bring such a conflagration upon his people. Certainly not over a Terran maid. The best course of action was to flee, and hope Ferra'leen was not up to a chase.

\* \* \* \* \*

Torture. That's all Selena knew. And everything, including the landscape around her was a total blur. As was the golden god. His touch a distant memory.

*My dark prince.* She knew it was incomprehensible that he was real, but as the taut, muscle-clad buttocks rocked in time with his marathon pace just below her head, she knew nothing could be more real. Her fingers itched to slide across the flashing hip around to the throbbing bulge she'd felt pressed against her thighs just moments before. The thought alone brought a fresh wave of longing and she pressed her nails into her palm to keep from screaming. Fire continued to burn deep in her belly, and if she were able to free her hands, they would be working to relieve the vicious need that consumed her.

But right now her arms were pinned to her side as she hung upside down over his sculpted shoulder. Despair washed through her, fueled by confusion. *What's happening to me?* Silver-white flashes zinged by her head, and Selena felt their speed increase as warm air rushed by her bare body.

Another mental command erupted in her head. *Breathe deeply then hold!*

Selena complied, her mind too fuzzy to question the order. The instant she sucked in a lungful of green-scented air, her world shifted. It felt as if they had penetrated a barrier, heavy and thick, before popping through to the other side. Color, sharp and fractured filled the space around her, and somehow Selena managed to hold her breath despite a wave of nausea that punched her in the stomach.

*Do not breathe!* came the unassailable husky voice in her mind.

Selena closed her eyes to the writhing colors. Painful pricks of light flickered behind her eyelids, and Selena knew she was close to losing consciousness. And when she did, her mouth would open and in would come whatever permeated the disturbing space.

Selena's hands knotted into fists against the dark prince's pumping muscles.

*A moment more,* mi'Awen, *only a moment...*

*Right. No problem*, thought Selena her blood thrumming violently, her lungs on fire. Blotches of black teased the edges of her mind, and a numbing calm called to Selena. *Release...let go...*

And despite her determination not to, Selena felt a part of herself reach for the promised release. But it wasn't blissful peace that filled her. Darkness, foul and razor-edged, sent her spinning into emptiness.

## Chapter Five

"No!" Serosen felt the maid's body give way to the strain. As the woman drew the sacred path's essence into her lungs, her body jerked against his shoulder, and Serosen cursed Ferra'leen to a thousand hells.

The egress into his Kingdome lay ahead, but there was no time. Spying the rust-colored slash to his right, Serosen twisted, and saying the necessary words, passed through the viscous barrier into the ginger beams of an autumn sunrise. He lowered the maid into the waving goldenrod and stripped off his pouch.

Her heart-shaped face was deathly pale, her pink lips parted, yet no air passed in or out of their inviting depths. An unfamiliar stab found his heart.

Only the strongest could brave the passageways that connected the worlds of fey. The paths were once well used by those in power, but the magick that made up the corridor was deteriorating back to its original, wild state. Despite the elders working to reweave the ancient magicks, it continued to decay, with threads of feral energies bleeding into the Kingdomes in which it crossed.

For someone completely unwarded and untrained as a Terran to use the path was certain suicide. But Serosen had been confident in his ability to ward the maid at least temporarily, while he passed through to his own Kingdome, as long as she didn't draw any of the wild energy into her body.

But she had. And as Serosen looked down on her inert form, he realized he might be too late.

Firmly placing doubt aside, he stripped off his tunic, retrieved a small vial from his pouch and emptied the contents onto his palms. Tingling raced through his hands and up his arms as he rubbed them together, uttering the *Bricht*, ancient words to activate the potent organics. His body quaked with the energy his words and the oil amassed, and with single-minded determination, he straddled the beautiful Terran and placed a hand on each side of her face.

"You will not have her, *Balor*," he whispered, before gripping the maid's head in his hands and covering her still lips with his own.

\* \* \* \* \*

Lightning shattered the darkness and Selena screamed. A shimmer of blue rippled before her, painfully bright in the heart of the blackness. She felt a pull, drawing her toward the light, and yet another part of her remained anchored to the ice cold and ever-tightening void.

"Please…" Selena begged, her hand reaching for the spark of blue, right before she was yanked backward with stunning force. Selena spiraled down a tunnel rippled with a sickening crimson glow. Her hands scrabbled for purchase, anything solid to slow her descent.

*Let go of the fear…* came a voice, soft and far away.

Awash in the blood red glow, Selena moaned in terror.

*The fear is what holds you. Acknowledge it, then look beyond. Find me.*

A spark of irritation flared. "No problem," Selena growled at the disembodied voice. "Nix the fear. Piece of cake."

She could have sworn she heard a chuckle, deep and melodious. *Anger. That may work as well.*

Fire burned in Selena at her dark prince's words. Hell yes, she was angry. Bits and pieces of what had transpired as of late flashed through her mind's eye. Gwendolyn's party: something she hadn't really wanted to attend because she knew Curt, Gwen's lying, womanizing son-of-a-bitch brother would be there. But she'd had to go, for Gwen's sake.

*What an opportunity*, her blonde and buxom best friend since sixth grade had said. Two weeks in Britain seeing the sights, and then one last road trip to attend a monster grad party on, of all places, a windswept Scottish moor in the middle of no-wheresville.

So Selena had gone, and the two weeks before Gwen's graduation from St. Andrews had been memorable as they traveled Great Britain on the Brit Rail. Studious and serious by nature, Gwen had been a fascinating tour guide, but within days, Serena longed for a noisy Tempe streetside café that served sizzling carnitas and super-sized mango margaritas. Not to mention some skin-roasting sunshine, and the heady aroma of mesquite, blooming citrus, and sage. Anything but the damp, gray and dreary countryside.

Then came the party.

Selena remembered a winding trip through a blinding green countryside. Once parked, they *hiked* another twenty minutes, arriving at a monster bonfire surrounded by clusters of whooping students. Gwen had explained that the Ancient History grads were emulating the Celtic subjects they'd been studying for the past two years. Selena had been amazed at the wild body paint and costumes they were wearing—or more accurately, *not* wearing.

*Bunch of flakes*, was Selena's take, but at least they had a keg of decent brew and there was an electric energy in the air that was undeniably erotic. Of course, Curt was there. His hands had been all over the ass of a sheet-wrapped druid with Medusa braids. It hurt—still—but after a few pints, the pain had lessened, and with the music in full throb, Selena had been able to lose herself in the indigenous rhythms.

The nearly hedonistic atmosphere had been interesting, to say the least, and Selena recalled how shocked she was that uptight Gwen would even think of attending such a bash, when she heard *the voice*. Like a magnetic pull, she'd spun out of the gyrating circle of students and trailed his summons. Up the dark moor, through a thick stand of ash, to an oval standing stone. He stepped out from behind it, a winsome smile on his angelic face.

Selena's recollections suddenly became foggy at that point, and she grasped for the flow with which the previous memories had sped. But only fragments remained, leaving the dark moor and stepping into a bright summer day. Green grass, cool upon her back. The golden god, naked, above her, and that all-consuming need...

*Until my dark prince.*

Sizzling light burned behind her eyelids and the stench of ozone and smoldering flesh assailed her. Selena gagged.

*What he did…the power he held…the supernatural flight…*
*He saved me. Twice.*

The conclusion rocked Selena and her eyes opened on the reality that currently consumed her. She continued to fall, red ripples now mere slashes in the perpetual midnight as she picked up speed.

"Enough!" she screamed into the void. "I've had it! Kill me if you want, but I'll be damned if I'm going to fall another freakin' inch!"

She stopped. On a dime, suspended in the crimson and black tunnel, her outstretched arms pale and glowing. The sensation left her stomach up in her throat, but even so, Selena sighed with relief, until she looked up—into oblivion.

Dread wormed its way into her chest. *How do I get back?*

*The dark prince.*

*Look for me*, isn't that what he'd said? Selena raised her head and cried, "Where are you?"

Ominous laughter filled the space around her.

"Hello?" Selena ventured, her legs waving beneath her as if she were treading water, her hair spreading out around her body. A name, a name…what had it been? Something with an S. Serosen. *That was it.*

Selena licked dry lips. "S-Serosen? Is that you?"

A form materialized before her, and Selena reared back. It was a man, tall and dark, but not her prince. He hovered only inches away, a furtive smile on his aquiline face.

"No, certainly *not* your dark prince." A subtle shimmer of gray emanated from his body in waves. "But I could be, if you come with me, Selena."

Selena sucked in a breath. "How-how do you know my name?"

Another chuckle and Selena was fascinated by his magnetic presence. He was handsome, in a sharp and slightly disturbing way, but there was something else...

"I know quite a bit about you, my dear. It's my duty to know, after all."

Dread amassed in Selena's gut. "I just want to get the hell out of here," she said, her tone not nearly as strong as she'd intended.

"Ah." He waved a hand and the tunnel disappeared. They stood in a field of waving blue cornflowers under a butter yellow sun. The stranger bowed at the waist. "Your wish is my command, milady."

A warm and fragrant breeze caressed Selena's bare body, tightening her nipples. She placed an arm over her exposed breasts. "Oh," she sighed, disorientated and slightly dizzy.

The stranger stepped closer, and with his nearness a wedge of nausea tickled the back of Selena's throat.

As his gaze fell upon her upturned face, Selena recoiled. *His eyes.* A gray, viscous fluid rippled on their surface like storm clouds boiling in a sea of oil.

*Death.* That's what the stranger was.

With a grin on his handsome face he reached out a steady hand. "Come to me, Selena. Your dream begins now and never ends."

Despite her revulsion, despite the tendrils of panic gripping her, she felt herself respond. *"Oh, God,"* Selena moaned mentally, *"I am lost, lost…"* She stepped toward Death's outstretched palm, her fingers dangling limply in the perfectly false warming rays.

Something stepped between them.

"No, you are not lost, *mi'Awen*."

A jolt rocked her, and Selena looked up. "You came," she whispered through near frozen lips. "You came for me."

Blue sizzled from the spirals and symbols that wound his powerfully built arms, across his neck and cheek, leaving him a ghostly, bare-chested glowing figure in the false spring-like landscape. He turned and inclined his head toward the more solid form standing behind him. "Are you working for Garethan now, Balor? You know you cannot touch one who is bonded. You have no claim over this maid."

The creature—for now that is what he seemed—no longer truly a man, nor a monster, but an amalgamation of the two—smirked and raised a chiseled brow. "That would be true indeed…*if* she were actually bonded."

As he turned back, a sly grin stole across her dark prince's features. "It has already begun." His words echoed through Selena's soul, darkening the world around them, and bringing a distinct longing back into Selena's core. But was it real? Was *he* real?

Everything spun as if on an axis, and all became a blur except for Serosen's face and his arresting eyes—hungry, grazed her body as he leaned in.

His breath, warm and spicy, caressed her parted lips. "I take you into myself, *mi'Awen*. I claim your soul as my own, your heart as my heart, your life above my life. With this joining we are of one mind. One spirit. Not parted even in death."

His lips touched hers to an explosion of light and color, and Selena knew with a certainty her dark prince had indeed arrived.

## Chapter Six

*So close to being lost to me.*

Serosen slammed into his physical form, his lips still pressed against...*Selena's*. He knew her name now. Felt it, like a firewhit's kiss upon his soul. Now to lure her back into her own body.

He knew he had to work fast, for to fumble in the Dark Lord's domain was to court disaster of the permanent kind. He had successfully drawn her away, but now he had to bring her all the way back.

And there was only one way to win her freedom—bond her to him, and he to her—for all eternity. Whereas the thought should have left him apprehensive and distraught, it instead filled him with a heady sense of power that nearly robbed him of his breath.

He deepened his kiss, and her lips yielded beneath his. Serosen probed their honeyed depths before trailing his tongue down her neck. He stopped at the now pulsating hollow at the base of her throat. *Her breath has returned.* And with it, Selena shifted beneath him, the tips of her luscious breasts hardening against his bare chest.

Serosen groaned and even with the need for haste, took the time to gaze upon the breath-taking body of his soulmate-to-be. Her golden skin glistened under the autumn sun, and her gently curved hips invited his eyes to travel past the strip of auburn hair to the moist region between her legs. As if anticipating his need, her legs eased apart, providing him a more intimate view of her glistening wetness.

His breath caught in his throat, and with unnatural quickness, he shed his boots and breeches. Serosen ran a hand down the length of his throbbing cock, a rumble building within his chest. How much sweeter it would be if the maid were fully aware of what they were about to consummate. Of his deep, almost animal need for her.

A hand suddenly brushed over his, before traveling down to the swollen tip of his staff. He gasped as the maid's slim fingers tightened ever-so-slightly, before caressing the pearly drop of semen on the head of his cock.

His gaze moved to her face—and her eyes—brilliant blue, were open and staring. She smiled, and Serosen was devastated by the flame of her beauty. His Tuatha vision could *see* the profundity of her spirit burning like a pure crystalline sky.

"I am here, my dark prince. Take me. Make me yours," she whispered, and the music of her words shattered Serosen's tightly reined control. His tattoos began to glow, not the violet blue of approaching danger, but a deep, cerulean blaze of passion.

Serosen didn't stop to question how Selena had managed to return to him without their consummation first…it was enough that she was here. And wanted him. Purely from her own volition. Not because of a spell. Or need of escape. She desired him as much as he needed her.

Selena's gaze traced the Oghms that twined around the left side of his body as he lowered himself. Her nipples rubbed sensually against his chest as his rock-hard length pressed against her taut belly. "Welcome me into your sacred region, Selena," Serosen whispered as he trailed his hand up her inner thigh, pausing only a moment at the strip of fine hair, before finding the moist warmth of her slit. The maid cried out, her legs spreading wider as Serosen teased the swollen nub. Her back arched, and he plunged his finger into its tight recess.

"Oh God," she groaned, her quim quivering around his now thrusting finger. "I-I'm going to—"

Serosen touched his lips to hers. "Come for me, *mi'Awen*. Let me feel your release."

"Oh…my…God…" the maid choked out as Serosen twisted his finger just so, his own breath ragged. Nails dug into his back as her scream split the silence. Somehow Serosen managed to hold back his own release as Selena's quim contracted around his drenched finger. She collapsed into him, and Serosen lowered himself just enough to cradle her flushed and trembling body.

Her breath, sweet, like orange blossom nectar, brushed his neck as she repeatedly called out to her God. Serosen felt a twinge of disquiet. He'd have to make certain his new soulmate didn't bring disaster upon their heads by summoning up more Gods than he could safely handle.

His own need throbbed greatly, and Serosen knew they had to complete the act of full joining. Their strong passion had broken Balor's hold on Selena, but without a true union, he could yet challenge Serosen's claim. Serosen lifted his head and ran his hand down the side of Selena's flushed face. Which is when he saw her gaze…focused wide on *his* face, as ferocious as a gryphon protecting its young.

*"What in the holy hell is going on?"* she said through clenched teeth, her chest rising and falling tantalizingly with each breath.

A tickle of amusement, and then unease filled Serosen when he realized the maid was truly free of enchantment. Her eyes were clear, their fire evident, and a niggling of fear lurked in their midnight depths. She was free of his cousin's spell. Free of the confusion she'd labored under since arriving in his world.

*Goddess…this might prove difficult*, thought Serosen.

\* \* \* \* \*

*Ohmygod. My dark prince. Above me. Our legs entwined. His finger! His finger still deep inside…*

Which he flicked, ever-so-slightly. Selena gasped, a rush of fresh desire surging through her, despite the fact that she'd just had the most amazing orgasm of her life.

*This isn't happening, this isn't happening*, Selena chanted to herself as she tried to process the multiple sensations assaulting her. Again, his finger teased, twisted in such a way that Selena's hips began to grind against his hand of their own volition. Wanting more, wanting —

As if reading her thoughts, his silky dark head dipped and captured a puckered nipple. His tongue danced over the sensitive tip, circling, sucking, rolling the pebbled bud in his warm mouth. A shaft of pure pleasure knifed through Selena. She moaned and bucked against Serosen, knowing in that moment that she'd never be able to resist. She wanted him…all of him, deep inside her. It didn't matter where she was, or what had gone before. It was only *him*. His body linked with hers. His mouth, hot and demanding laving her breasts, his skillful finger dipping in and out of her pussy.

"More," she heard herself whimper. "I need more of you." She lifted a hand to his chiseled jaw, running the tips of her fingers up to the perfectly sculpted flesh of his ear, stopping at its pointed ridge. She felt him gasp and shudder against her. A firm hand gripped hers, and gently pulled it down to his chest.

"My sweet," he growled, "even a Night Ranger can maintain only so much control."

Selena flushed at the sultry tone of his voice, thick with passion. "Then don't," she whispered, her hand running down his chest, over rippling abs, to grasp the base of his massive, rigid cock. "Let go."

Their eyes met, and Selena gasped as an inner light flared behind the gunmetal surface. His face broke into an almost feral smile, before his head dipped and his lips captured hers in a demanding, soul-wrenching kiss. Selena surrendered to his probing tongue, fire igniting along every nerve in her body.

And a small measure of alarm.

*What have I gotten myself into?*

All fear fled as he lifted her clear of the ground in an instant, spinning her onto her hands and knees—holding her there, by a strong arm encircling her waist. Which was good, as every muscle in Selena's body was quivering nearly uncontrollably with anticipation. His mouth, hot, began trailing kisses on the nape of her neck, then down her back, as his other hand caressed her bare ass, narrowly avoiding the drenched folds of her exposed pussy.

Selena groaned, her fingers digging into fragrant loam, its earthy scents filling her senses. It was disturbing and highly erotic, not being able to see her seducer. Not being able to tell what he was about to do next.

As his tongue painted spirals on her lower back, his hand slid along her inner thighs, coming tantalizingly close to that secret part of her that was screaming for his possessive touch. "Please," whimpered Selena.

Serosen's warm breath tickled Selena's slit. "So beautiful, like a blushing rose, each fold leading the eye to its enticing heart."

Her back arched and she cried out as her dark prince's tongue flicked against her clit, then teased at her wet folds. Pressure blossomed at Selena's core, and she knew she was on the brink of another orgasm. *How could anything feel so good? So right?*

Suddenly the tongue was gone, and Selena protested its abrupt absence. In an instant his breath was on the nape of her neck, his chest pressed to her back as his hand cupped a throbbing breast. "What do you want, Selena?" He gently rolled her nipple between finger and thumb, sending bolts of electricity zinging throughout her body. "Tell me what you want of me."

Selena groaned, her ass pushing against his cock. "I want you to fuck me. Bury your hard c—"

Before she could finish, Serosen's hands gripped her hips, and in one massive thrust, his cock parted her wet folds. He held still within her, and Selena ground her hips.

She could feel his breath hot upon her neck. "How do you want me to fuck you, Selena?"

"Hard, hard and fast," she choked out, her legs trembling. "Please…"

He thrust once, and Selena screamed with the pleasure of it.

"And what else, *mi'Awen?*" He placed a hand on her ass, squeezing firmly. "Hard and fast, and what else?"

Selena bit her lower lip, her pussy close to exploding around his penetrating shaft.

"Oh God, deep, I want to feel you deep inside me."

"As you wish," he growled in her ear. With the power of his muscled thighs, he thrust deep and Selena screamed as her orgasm took her. Blood pounded in her ears as the contractions came, one after the other.

Her lover held perfectly still as the waves of ecstasy claimed her. Selena could feel the entire length and width of him filling her. "Oh...my...God."

Serosen bent close to her ear. "No more talk of Gods, *mi'Awen*. It is just you and I, now, at this moment." And he began to plunge into her, slowly at first, each powerful stroke bringing her once more back to the edge of bliss. *How could he have so much control?* Selena marveled. She'd already orgasmed how many times? Twice?

*Faster.* His hands tightened on her hips, pulling her into his thrusts. *Harder.* Selena matched his pace, back arched, head tipped back, her hands pushing against the ground to allow him even deeper into her core.

Lights began to swim behind her eyelids as the pressure built and his thrusts became more demanding. His balls slapped against her clit and Selena moaned, "Yes, God, yes."

Serosen's powerful voice filled her head. *"I take all of you,* mi'Awen, *as I give you all of myself, so shall we be bonded, forever and even unto the other side."*

Selena felt an unusual tingling join the other heightened vibrations within her. Something more than passion. More than lust. It was an inner fire—a luminosity, spreading from the heat of their joined loins, into every channel of her heart, then on to her head, until every inch of her was filled with the potent, intoxicating sensation.

And, she realized, she was not alone in her thoughts, perceptions, body. Selena felt not just Serosen buried within her, but *in* her—literally—and she in him. His thrusting hips, the way her hot, slick pussy encased his throbbing cock. The fact that he was oh-so-close to spilling himself deep into her womb.

The double awareness consumed her, and as her body and mind stretched to accommodate the veracity of the experience, she felt Serosen's breath quicken, his body pounding out a manic rhythm, his heart thrumming in perfect time with her own.

Her world exploded as the orgasm rocked her. But even as contractions flooded her, Selena rode Serosen to his own release. She felt it amass from a place other than just increased blood flow. Like a frothing ball of liquid light, it shattered them, cording both of their bodies upon the leaf-strewn carpet of gold.

His arms tightened around her protectively as they lay spent. Selena had never felt more secure. The musk of their sex enveloped her as well as the rich, earthy scents of the woods surrounding them, and within moments Selena collapsed willingly into darkness.

## Chapter Seven

A tickle of apprehension prodded Serosen. His eyes flew open to —

Whoops and giggles and shrieks. More joined in as Serosen turned his head, the only part of his body that he *could* turn.

*I slept! How could I have passed into sleep without warding us first?*

*Damnation.*

Brownies. Hundreds of them, mayhap thousands. One could never be too certain with the woodland sprites — they blended into the flora and fauna almost as well as the wood nymphs.

Serosen didn't need to test each limb to know he and Selena, whose back was tight to his chest and belly, were tied to each other, and the ground, by thousands of near-invisible threads. Threads painstakingly gathered by the brownies, from the *Kenoch* spiders. Practically unbreakable by brute strength or by magick, as they held a natural enchantment of their own.

*Damnation again,* thought Serosen as he glared at the twisting, celebrating sprites only inches from his head. Ragged tufts of hide covered their most sensitive parts, and each thrust either a twisted spear of gray ash or tiny bow with needle thin arrows into the air. Harmless, if they'd not been tipped with *Kenoch* poison. Several pricks could drop a unicorn into a deep slumber.

Not harmful to an elf, 'less he be pricked by thousands at once—a distinct possibility from the situation he'd allowed himself and his soulmate to be subjected to. And as a Terran, it would take much less to stop Selena's fragile heart.

Tendrils of webbing tugged around his ankles as little fingers plucked at the silvery threads like lyre strings. He twitched a toe, sending the riotous group squealing backward. His eyes trailed the whooping horde. As far as Fey Folk went, brownies were a primitive species— singular in their self-gratifying devotion to whatever they found interesting or fascinating at the moment. They served no one and nothing but their own sense of entertainment or pleasure, which made them impossible allies, bothersome if relatively harmless enemies, and quite ignorable as long as you never allowed yourself to be captured by them.

As Serosen had mindlessly done. And there was no telling how long they had lain unconscious and unaware beneath the tangled web, as once trussed by brownies, time slows for those captured. It had at least been an entire night and well into another day, by the looks of things.

Serosen gritted his teeth, and tried not to utter a curse upon the brown beasties. There was also no reasoning with the tiny creatures, and yet, he dared not use his own magick to destroy them. Fey Folk they were, and protected by the woodland spirits, who would certainly retaliate should he singe them to bits. Selena and he would likely escape, but at what cost? The woodland spirits would cry foul to their protector, King Fash'en, who happened to be his father's cousin. The last thing his father needed to deal with at this turbulent time.

*Three damnations!*

Serosen sighed and worked to formulate a plan. At least Selena was still deep in slumber. Being that the brownies were easily agitated, it would not bode well for his new bride to wake fully unenchanted to see thousands of savage creatures cavorting around her naked body.

The mere thought of Selena's unclothed, luscious form curled against his brought an instant rise to his manhood. He was painfully aware of her bare breasts rising and falling with each breath beneath his arm. Her round buttocks pressed into the curve of his thigh.

It took a deep breath and tight control to quell his desire, and still, he could not keep his thoughts from their coupling. It had been...extraordinary. Unlike anything he'd ever experienced, and he'd experienced much in his five-hundred years. Incalculable methods of pleasure — and sweet anguish — yet none had equaled the powerful sensations and climax of joining with the Terran.

The realization left him perplexed. And there had been something else about his new bride that had concerned him, but with brownies squealing in his ear, he was unable to piece together exactly what it had been.

"What in the holy hell are *those*?" came a fierce whisper.

Serosen jerked free of his reverie, drawing multiple pairs of bark-brown eyes in their direction. The whooping stopped. The dancing ended.

Was he to have not a single reprieve from this unconscionable day?

Selena tensed against him. "You think *your* day has been unconscionable?"

Which was when Serosen recalled one of the things that had troubled him about his new bride. *She has been able to read my thoughts without my permission.* Du'an's enchantment hadn't allowed for that.

*How is that possible?*

"How is *any* of this possible?" Selena tried to twist around, but only succeeded in scrunching herself tighter into Serosen's groin. "Answer me that, buster!"

Serosen quickly warded his thoughts and grinned, which he was thankful Selena could not see, as he was certain it would only incense her more. The Terran had fire...something she would need to survive in *Tir na n-Og*.

For there was no question of her going home. Not now that she had been bonded to Tuathan royalty. With minimal movement, Serosen leaned into Selena, his body shielding as much of her as possible.

"Do not speak aloud, *mi'Awen*. We find ourselves at some risk from the creatures that have captured us. Do not agitate them, lest they prick us into unconsciousness — or worse."

The brownies padded closer, their weapons at the ready. Serosen felt Selena's sharp intake of breath as the creatures began to pluck at her burgundy tresses. Their twittering voices were lost on Serosen's ears. The brownie language was near impossible for even the most skillful linguists to interpret. He could only hope they would tire and find amusement elsewhere, providing him enough time to liberate them from the *Kenoch* webbing.

*"What are they?"* came Selena's strained thoughts.

*"Brownies,"* Serosen answered through elf-speak. *"Harmless, essentially. Unless they manage to capture you in numbers,"* he added reluctantly, finding it difficult to hold anything back from the Terran.

He felt her twitch against him as the small, brown hands touched the flesh of her rounded, shell-shaped ears—so unlike that of most fey. *"Why have they captured us?"*

*"For their amusement...and because my complete negligence allowed it."*

*"Well, what are we going to do about it?"*

Serosen couldn't help but smile at Selena's practical response. It was certain any average Terran would be in hysterics. But Serosen had realized from the first moment he laid eyes on his soulmate that she was no ordinary Terran.

*"We tolerate their prodding, then wait for them to tire of us. Fortunately, they have a very short attention span."*

He felt Selena humph, and he imagined he could see her azure eyes flashing daggers at the diminutive beasts.

"Hey! Leave off you dirty little freak!"

Selena's screech split the air, along with a violent shake of her body, which sent brownies flinging and shrieking in several directions at once. One bounced off Serosen's shoulder. Another tumbled into the crevice between their bodies.

*Centaurs balls,* thought Serosen.

Selena was quaking, her chest rising and falling rapidly against his arm. "The little perverts were sticking fingers where they had no business sticking them!"

Serosen made quick work of the brownie wedged between Selena's back and his chest, applying just enough pressure to render it unconscious, and its spear merely another twig on the ground beneath them.

"That was not a wise move, my sweet," Serosen murmured in Selena's ear, "however well deserved."

As the brownies regrouped around the pair, more filtered out of the woods to surround them. Tittering and shrieking, the sprites raised their spears and bows, brown eyes blazing.

"Uh, I guess this is what you meant by agitated?" Selena said, her toes digging into the ground at their feet.

"Uh-hum," murmured Serosen as he desperately tried to formulate a spell that would incapacitate the brownies without harming them.

Several jerkily advanced, spears thrusting. Selena shrank as far back against Serosen as she could.

"Why don't you just fry them with whatever you used on those other monsters?"

Serosen clenched his teeth as pricks pierced his calves. "Not-a-viable-option."

*A sleep spell...a sleep spell...why didn't I pay attention to non-lethal charms in early training?*

A fearsome rumble exploded from the dense, autumn woods. Then a massive roar sent brownies screeching and scattering. Twig-limbs scrabbled, leaping up and over the bound pair. Heedless of where they stepped in their haste to escape, hundreds of tiny bodies sped in every direction.

Serosen focused on the source of the brownies' sudden terror. Underbrush rattled and branches snapped — then with a fearsome crash, the beast broke into the clearing, flinging brownies to the four winds like so many mosquitoes.

## Chapter Eight

"Holy Mother of God," Selena whispered aloud. If she could have crossed herself, she would have. It was the biggest freaking bear she had ever seen. Giant wasn't an adequate word to describe the golden-haired beast. Its head alone must have been three feet across, and its mouth—its *teeth*—easily the length of her hand was snapping from side to side in an attempt to catch the fleeing brownies.

"We are chopped liver if you don't fry *this* brute," Selena choked out.

Serosen was dead-still behind her, and Selena wondered if he'd passed out. She wiggled her rear directly into his groin, and sighed with relief when he tensed and grunted.

His arm tightened around her chest. "Nay. I will certainly not…fry…this noble animal."

Selena's mouth fell open. *"What?* Are you insane?" Surely he'd lost his mind, or *wanted* to be ripped to shreds and eaten alive.

Having successfully driven off the miniature horde without actually consuming any of them, the mutant bear advanced on the bound pair. Selena could think to do nothing else but pray. Which she did, in earnest, including in that prayer the fact that God was welcome to pluck her out of this nightmare and put her back into her boring, average life at any moment. Preferably soon—like *now*.

She couldn't tear her eyes away from the stunning beast. Its fur shimmered in the autumn sun, its movements graceful, despite its bulk. At least it was no longer growling. Its large, black nose twitched and sniffed as if to analyze their tenderness level, prior to his first taste as he lumbered closer.

Selena's eyes widened as the bear leaned in with his massive, shaggy head, its deep, brown eyes boring directly into hers. Words stuck in her throat, and her heart thumped so hard Selena knew it would be the first thing the creature ripped from her body. As the beast reared back, Selena closed her eyes. *This is it. I'm on my way to see Tia Sophia.*

Air buffeted the entire length of her body, and with it, a thousand *pinging* noises. Like guitar strings plucked along a top fret. An airy *whomp* soon followed, and Selena realized that her dark prince's arm was no longer draped protectively around her chest. She opened her eyes to a very large, very wet nose pressed close to her cheek.

Selena scrabbled backward. "*Dio mios!*"

The bear sat on its haunches, tongue lolling like a playful hound.

Selena shakily got onto her feet, arms covering her bare breasts. With her heart still hammering, she tore her eyes away from the beast to look for Serosen. He stood beside her, a grim look on his darkly handsome face.

Serosen nodded toward the bear. "Truly, I will owe you a thousand life debts my friend before either of us reach our golden years."

*Okay, he's talking to a bear*, thought Selena, lips pursed. Maybe the little fairies had poisoned him after all.

A rumble bubbled up from the bear's chest, and to Selena's shock, it began to shimmer, then *change*. Fur shrank. Bulk diminished. Teeth disappeared, until a man remained, crouched upon the forest floor where the bear once sat. Selena blinked rapidly, a shallow buzzing filling her ears.

The man stood, and Selena couldn't help but trail his body with her eyes, from his bare feet, up his muscled calves and thighs, past his barely concealed, hide covered loins to a most remarkable chest, past what looked like a necklace of reddish bear claws around his neck—then on to his arresting, chiseled face, stopping at his deep-set brown eyes. *The exact same eyes as the bear.*

"My brother, there is never any debt between us. And we have many lifetimes to satisfy the Gods that the twining of our fates is deserved."

"It—how—" Selena twisted to Serosen. "Okay, now what is *he*?" she asked, jerking a thumb over her shoulder.

Her dark prince's eyes roamed her body, much as she had just done to the bear…er…man. Heat rushed to her face at the frank hunger in his steel-gray eyes, and Selena was instantly reminded of the incredible passion they had shared.

He stood before her completely bare. His beautiful, muscle-corded arms framed a sculpted chest, narrow waist and rock-hard abs, leading to his fully erect cock. Moisture flooded her swollen clit, and Selena knew her face was blushing hotter as a result of the potent onslaught of her attraction to… She glanced at his ears. Okay, *what exactly was he?*

Shoulder-length raven hair lifted ever-so-slightly as he stepped closer, and Selena backed away, her breath catching in her throat at the mere thought of his touch. Of his powerful hands caressing her aching breasts, teasing her now dripping pussy.

Which is when Selena realized she was still naked. She slapped hands onto her intimate parts—not that her arm covered more than a speck of her full breasts.

*Damn. Where are my clothes?* Selena thought as she scanned the clearing.

She stopped her frantic search, her gaze drawn once more to the impressive beast-man. He looked Native American, both in his features, and in the way in which he carried himself. His ears were not pointed like Serosen's, and his long black hair and tanned skin, while beautiful, did not hold the same ethereal quality as her dark prince, or any of the other bizarre creatures she'd seen so far.

He looked as if he'd just walked off the set of *Dances with Wolves*.

Selena found she was suddenly dizzy with the enormity of what had transpired in the past...what had it been? Four hours? Six? It felt like an eternity. And she understood none of it.

Her legs trembled and Selena knew she either had to sit or she would fall down. Before she could lower herself to the brightly colored forest floor, a warm hand clasped her arm and eased her down. She sank to her knees, her breath shivering out in shallow gasps. "I, uh, don't feel so well," she whispered, hating herself for being such a ninny.

Serosen sat beside her and motioned for the bear-man to do the same. He never released her arm, and the firm but gentle pressure of his hand comforted her. "You must have taken a few pricks from the brownies' spears. Do you feel dizzy? Is your chest heavy?" he asked, and it was as if his voice was several feet away instead of only inches.

Selena nodded, her hair brushing against her shoulders and back, reminding her all over again that she was naked as a jaybird—in the presence of two exceptionally virile...men...or whatever they were.

"Yes, and I just feel, well, weak," Selena admitted. Probably not the best thing to cop to under the circumstances.

A hand brushed hair away from her face, and as Serosen's fingers trailed across her cheek, electricity sang throughout her body, leaving her dizzier, but flushed with desire at the same time. *Oh God, am I reverting back to that never-get-enough nympho state?* thought Selena.

Serosen chuckled, and Selena looked up. As their gazes met, Selena felt that intoxicating pull once more—that sense of profound connection. Something her *Tia* Sophia would have called *fated*. But to Selena's ears, the term had always had too much in common with the word *fatal*. She had grown up determined to not let others predetermine her life or destiny, including God, although out of force of habit, Selena still hung loosely to her Catholic roots—the saints, the rituals and rules. Not that she did very well with the rules, but the traditions were too deeply ingrained for her to ignore completely what her beloved aunt had tried to impart to her.

"Nothing about the past hours of my life have been a laughing matter," Selena murmured, her eyes still locked with her lover's.

Serosen's expression sobered, and as he cupped the back of Selena's neck, her entire body relaxed into his palm. "This is true, *mi'Awen*, and I am sorry if you felt I mocked what you have endured. Nothing could be further from the truth. For I, more than anyone, understand the enormity of what has transpired."

The gravity in his voice sparked apprehension in Selena's belly, and despite her dizziness and fatigue, she straightened and focused on his striking face. "Where am I? And why am I here? I need to understand," Selena said firmly, "now."

Her dark prince's gaze flicked to the bear-man sitting across from them, who remained still, his body alert but at ease, his dark eyes watching them intently.

Serosen took both her hands, and Selena's attention was immediately drawn back to her dark prince. To his fiery touch upon her skin. To the pounding of her heart at the slightest contact between them.

"The only thing you need to know at this moment, *mi'Awen...*" He gently turned her arms palm up, and Selena gasped as her eyes lighted on alien-looking writing emblazed on the underside of both her wrists. "...is that we are bonded for eternity." Serosen turned his own arms slightly upward, revealing similar symbols on the insides of his supple wrists. "This bears the evidence of our joining—and the blessing of the Goddess that it be so."

He turned her hands over and clasped her arm just above the wrists so that their markings met. A concussive jolt slammed into Selena. *Fire*, liquid and sensuous, exploded from their joined arms driving the dizziness and lethargy from her body. Instantaneously, all of her senses sharpened. She could perceive each tree, bush, animal and creature hundreds of yards in every direction through the dense forest. Her ears effortlessly harkened each peep, leap and scrabble of mouse and ant. And other energies...palpitating within the heart of the wood.

It was heady, exhilarating and terrifying all in the same breath. As quickly as it enveloped her, the sensation ended as Serosen broke their connection. A throbbing indigo radiance danced around her dark prince's body. His expression was intense, and something else…surprise, maybe?

Selena looked down at her own arms, and nearly passed out when she realized that same light was emanating from her as well. Welling right out of her skin in waves that quickly dissipated as it wafted a few inches away from her body.

She stared at her alien lover, and for the first time in her twenty-three years of life, words failed her. Selena DeLaPava had nothing at all to say.

# Chapter Nine

Serosen gazed at his Terran bride. He'd had no doubt that Selena's skin would bear the bonding script of their union. But he'd had no idea that joining their *danu awen* would result in such a potent melding of their spiritual centers. In fact, Serosen had assumed a Terran's capacity to meld with one of fey origin to be limited.

He'd been witness to Tuathan and Terran unions in the past, and each had resulted in less than perfect pairings. Often the bond would endure until the Tuathan became bored or disenchanted with their new lover, and bargained a release from Goddess *Danu*. The Terran was then given the choice to return to earth, or remain in *Tir na n-Og* in the capacity of a non-magickal citizen.

Red Claw drew his eye, and Serosen wrenched his gaze away from Selena's glowing flesh to stare at his hunt brother. He raised a finely arched brow, and Serosen was quick to link their thoughts.

*"Brother, as you can see, much has transpired in the past few hours."*

Serosen felt Red Claws chuckle, though his lips betrayed not a hint. *"Yes, even a stubborn bear such as myself can see the truth in that statement."* His gaze lighted on Selena. *"She is...captivating. And though her aura sings of her Terran heritage, there is something else about her, my old friend, something...other. "*

He paused, and Serosen knew exactly what Red Claw was referring to. He'd sensed it in Selena as well—a distinctiveness that was not wholly Terran. Yet, what?

Red Claw drew a pouch from around his waist and opened it. *"Already the wind carries word of your union to the four Kingdomes, as well as a warning."* With nimble fingers, he pinched the dry contents and placed it in his open palm.

Selena, who had become as silent as a stone, raised her head to watch Red Claw work, and Serosen felt his heart shudder at the look of bewilderment on her arresting face. He had so much to explain, and not a moment of time to do it.

His friend spoke aloud, "I have seen the forces which even now seek to undo your union, my friends. I give you this blessing, so that your travel, while in peril, be swift and unerring, and that you arrive at your true destination like a blessed arrow to the heart of its enemy." He blew on his palm. Dust rose in a cloud to cover Serosen and Selena, the sparkles crackling like thousands of frenzied pixies. Serosen could feel the authority of the charm, and his tattoos pulsed in response.

Serosen didn't know the spelled herb Red Claw had used, but trusted in his friend's consummate herbal skill and foreknowledge. A shaman of high regard, Red Claw had passed freely amongst his people for as long as Serosen had been alive. With the closing of the earth gates two hundred years ago, Red Claw had chosen to stay in *Tir na n-Og*, in the hopes of seeing the gates one day reopened, so he could resume his travels and guardianship of his people.

But the way the winds were currently traveling, that wasn't likely to happen any time soon.

Serosen stood, pulling Selena up with him. He knew through the joining of their *danu awen* she was now free of the *Kenoch* poison, and it was essential that they begin their journey to his demesne.

He turned to eye the sacred path they'd passed through to enter the Autumn Kingdome. There was no question of them traveling through the portal again. The journey had to be overland, making the risks they would encounter from their opposition even greater.

Stepping forward, Serosen clasped arms with his hunt brother. "Many thanks for the blessing, Red Claw. With it we shall travel swiftly overland, and with great caution." Serosen knew his friend understood the risk involved in assisting he and Selena on their journey, but there was no doubt he would again when needed.

Red Claw released Serosen and moved to Selena. Her head tipped back, and her expression betrayed her fascination and apprehension. Red Claw reached out...waiting, giving her the choice to make the connection.

After a moment, Selena extended a sun-browned hand. She paused, her fingers a fraction away from Red Claw's. "Thank you, for saving our lives." Her hand disappeared within his, her eyes unwavering on his face. "It's not something I'm ever likely to forget."

They dropped hands and Red Claw backed away, a smile emblazoned on his strong-boned visage. "Nor I, sister." His gaze settled back onto Serosen. "Truly, you have chosen — or more accurately — fate has chosen for you a most enchanting companion, my friend." Then in elf-speak, *"Be wary, Serosen. Trouble brews, and somehow it is connected to your new bride. The signs are clouded as to how, or why, but I have no doubt that it is. There is a mystery to unravel here, and it's in everyone's best interest that it be solved quickly."*

"*Yes,*" returned Serosen. "*I've already encountered Ferra'leen's interference. Something is definitely afoot, and I have no intention of letting circumstances steal Selena from me.*" Serosen's gut tightened at the mere thought. After a deep breath to calm himself, he took Selena's hand. She stiffened at his touch, and Serosen reluctantly released her.

Mating with the woman was one thing. Getting Selena to trust him would be something else.

"How fares my family, Red Claw?" Serosen asked as they walked to the edge of the clearing, Selena trailing behind. Things had been tense when he'd left with Vigil to combat the intruders on their southern-most border, he could only imagine what the atmosphere was now with rumors of his new bride making the rounds.

Red Claw was quiet, his expression tense. "Your sister…is…restless."

Serosen grunted. "Nothing new about that. She'll be driving every last one of her guardians to deep meditation simply to keep from strangling her, I'm certain. What about Father?"

A sigh. "He despairs still, my friend. Things are not moving quickly enough to suit him. The council refuses to meet any sooner than the carefully set date, for fear the Unsellie Court will move to intercept."

"Bah! That's nonsense," Serosen said, shoving a hand through his hair. "It makes more sense to secretly plan an earlier session with only the top advisors present. Less risk to all."

Red Claw nodded, his long black hair waving forward to hide his face. "Yes. It seems obvious, but the Faerie

*Night Elves: Wicked Pleasures*

Court and those of the other Kingdomes seem set against it."

Anger seethed inside Serosen. Were they all blind? This was no time for political games. If ever there was a moment for the Kingdomes and Courts of fey to be unified, now was it. Why couldn't they all see that?

A cool hand on his arm brought his head around. Selena's brilliant azure eyes were clear, her lips pursed. "I wasn't a big Tolkien fan, but thank God I at least sat through the DVDs."

Serosen tried to focus on the meaning of her words, but hadn't a clue what his bride was referring to.

She continued. "I think I have some idea of where I might be, and maybe even how I got here, but what I want to know now is, how in the hell do I get back?" She directed the last part of her question to Red Claw. Her chin thrust out, and her hands went to her sensuous hips. "Tell me how to get home, and I'll be out of everyone's hair."

With a sober expression, Red Claw placed a hand upon Selena's shoulder. "Sister, what you ask is not possible. Not at this moment, anyway." His hunt brother dropped his hand, but his somber gaze stayed fixed on Selena. "But I will tell you this. If there should come a time where it is your greatest desire to return to earth, I shall find a way to take you."

A growl started in Serosen's throat and he nearly leapt upon his friend. *How could he say such a thing?* He and Selena must *not* be separated, not now, not ever!

Before he could wrap his hands around Red Claw's neck, his friend held up a palm. *"Calm yourself, brother. It was important that your bride hear those words. Place yourself in her body, Serosen. Everything is upside down from what she has been taught is reality. You must give her time to come to grips with what has been thrust upon her, and my words will offer her some security. And I have no doubt after she acclimates, her greatest wish will only be to stay by your side."*

Serosen found little comfort in his friend's words. What if Selena rejected their union completely? Red Claw would be obligated to return her. He was a man of his word. The thought made Serosen's stomach churn. His eyes narrowed, and friend or no, he realized with some shock, he would battle even Red Claw to keep Selena at his side.

Red Claw sighed and nodded. "So be it, my friend. Let's hope it never comes to that."

Before Serosen could utter another word, Red Claw stepped back and swiftly shape-shifted to his totem form. The giant golden bear swung his head side to side, uttering a series of grunts before bounding off into the dense underbrush.

Alone once more, Serosen couldn't help but turn his attention to his bride. Her body gleamed in the high sun, her hands having a hard time covering her large, succulent globes. Nothing would please Serosen more than for Selena to continue to walk around completely bare as the ladies of the Tuathan Court often did in their palaces and homes, but it wasn't practical for the journey ahead. Rugged terrain awaited them, as well as dangers unseen.

Not to mention his cock was hard as a rock at the mere sight of her. They'd never get anywhere at this rate.

Serosen went over to the pack Red Claw had left them at the edge of the clearing and withdrew a pair of supple, pale, *keffa*-silk breeches and an accompanying body-hugging tunic with generous laces at the front. As his fingers made contact with the clothes, Serosen instantly

*Night Elves: Wicked Pleasures*

sensed the spellwork woven into the seamless fabric. His sister's skillful mark was all over the beautiful yet rugged garments.

Serosen grunted his reluctant appreciation. He should have known his sister would find a way to wriggle a hand into his business—even from a Kingdome away. News had obviously traveled fast. He judged by the position of the sun, that he and Selena had been held captive for a night and half a day.

*Too much time…*Serosen worried. Red Claw had found them, but his hunt brother had extraordinary gifts of precognition, as well as an active network of woodland creatures and lower-level fey that constantly fed him information. But it wouldn't be long before the Unsellie mages were able to render a fix on their position. Selena's energies screamed of her world, but as Serosen strode toward his bride, he realized it was less so then the hours before their joining.

That was a good thing, if unusual.

He held the garments out. "For you, compliments of my sister, Eristta. They are lightweight, but exceptionally rugged and well-suited to any climate." And enchanted. But Serosen wasn't about to tell her that. Not yet.

Selena snatched them up and began dressing in earnest. He pulled on his own clothes and watched in fascination as her hair, rich and luxurious as the finest elfin silks, flowed around her face and shoulders as she bent to her task. When she'd finished and straightened, Serosen handed her a pair of matching boots.

She took them, her eyes narrowing as she inspected the footwear. "I imagine we're doing a lot of walking to get where we're going?"

"'Tis a certainty," he replied, his attention fastened on her generous bosom pushing against the laces of the tunic. His hand itched to cup the heavy mounds and run his thumbs over the hardened tips that were peeking through the tight fabric.

"And I'm supposed to do it in these?" She shook the boots by the soles. "They don't look thick enough to stand up to sand, let alone forest…and whatever else is out there."

Serosen pulled his eyes away from her breasts long enough to chuckle at her indignant expression. "*Mi'Awen*, trust me. The boots will protect your beautiful feet through burning desert or frozen field."

"Why do you call me that?" she asked breathlessly as she sat. "I suppose it means something along the lines of 'stupid woman' or 'foolish wench.'"

Somehow Serosen managed not to laugh, as it was clear by her tone that part of her was hoping those horrible things were *not* what he meant. He knelt beside her, his hand stilling her from pulling on the boots.

"Look at me, Selena." After a moment, she did, her chin trembling nearly imperceptibly under his gaze. "I know everything is strange and new, and I hope you can forgive me for not spiriting you away to a private location where we can learn everything there is to know about one another." He leaned in and placed a light kiss on the corner of her mouth, before drawing back. "You will have to find it within yourself to trust my judgment, my deep feeling for you and my passionate intentions that you come to no harm or insult—which includes my treatment of you."

*Night Elves: Wicked Pleasures*

With a huff, Selena shook off his hand and pulled on the boots. "You still didn't tell me what it—"

She stopped mid-sentence, and her eyes widened. She wiggled her toes and rubbed her hand along the inside and outside of the boots. Her forehead furrowed, and Serosen had to resist an urge to place a kiss upon the adorable crinkles. "These boots are like a second skin. As if they were custom made for me, just like the clothes."

Serosen took her hand and pulled her up. "They were, in a fashion." He urged her forward. "How do they feel?"

Selena's expression went from consternation to astonishment. "I—they...are wonderful. It's the oddest thing. It's as if I can feel the earth beneath my feet, almost like I'm barefoot, but without any sensation of, well, you know, the stuff that would be uncomfortable. Rocks, crunchy grass, uneven ground." Her eyes fastened on his. "How is that—" She threw up her hands. "Okay, I'm not going to keep sounding like a freakin' broken record. It's obvious that this—place doesn't operate under the same rules as good old earth. I'd sure like to understand a little more about it."

Serosen slung the bag of supplies that had held Selena's clothes over his shoulder, before turning at the sound of her impatient huff.

"That was your clue to spill, big guy," she growled, fists back onto her hips.

He grinned. He had no idea what she meant, but she was so adorable when she was irritated. Serosen hadn't thought he'd ever find anger in a mate an endearing quality. "I assume you wish more information, and there will be time for that. But not here. I promise to teach you all you need to know to live comfortably among the Fey Folk."

She blinked her striking eyes a few times, as if determining whether or not to work herself into a fit. Deciding it must not be worth the effort, she dropped her arms and gave a toss of her fiery hair. "Right. Eventually. Can I at least assume when you say "fey", you're referring to all the people…creatures in this world?"

Frowning, Serosen motioned for Selena to follow him. "No. There are…those who are not considered fey."

She fell into step beside him as they entered the shadowed forest. "Like Red Claw? He's Native American, isn't he? From my world?"

*Smart woman.* Serosen nodded. "Yes, but Red Claw is no ordinary Terran. He transcended his humanness many years ago through his own supernatural gifts combined with his shamanic practices. He resides in *Tir na n-Og* to maintain his fleshly body. Were he to travel strictly on the upper planes, his flesh would fade away, and he would become nothing but a spirit. Still powerful, but without the desire and ability to truly impact the lives of his people and their future."

"And what about me?" Selena asked, and Serosen detected a note of derision in her voice. "Am I just an ordinary Terran?"

He stopped, a quickening of his heart telling him how vital it was that Selena grasp how important she was to him. The difficult part being that *he* was as yet unsure how to deal with the strong, nearly overpowering emotions he felt for his new bride.

So why use words?

Serosen took Selena's chin and captured her lips. His soulmate began to pull away, but he deepened his kiss, his tongue snaking out to dance within the inner recesses of her mouth. Serosen felt her body surrender against his, her breasts pushing against his chest as she leaned in. Fire wicked through his groin, and with his other hand he cupped her ass and pulled her tight against his throbbing cock.

She gasped into his mouth, and Serosen shook with the intensity of their passion. With great restraint, he broke the kiss, his hand still gripping her chin. "Never ordinary, *mi'Awen*—my inspiration, my spirit, my heart." It was only a whisper, but Serosen felt as if he had shouted it clear to the ends of the Kingdome. "There is destiny at work in our union, my sweet, and somehow we must discover why we have been fated to spend eternity together."

Selena's eyes widened, and her luscious lips fell open. *"What?"*

With both hands she pushed away, then landed a blow on Serosen's chest. Her eyes flashed. "Eternity my sweet ass," she growled.

Serosen rubbed his neck, wondering how in Pandora's chest he'd ever be able to speak to his new bride without causing her to want to roast him over an open pit—with dragon wood for kindling.

## Chapter Ten

*Who does this* – fey *person think he is?* Selena turned on her heel and stalked off. Being so close to Serosen's gorgeous, powerfully built body was not conducive to maintaining her outrage and scorn.

Bound for eternity? Not hardly.

Her lips still burned from his kiss, and a surge of wetness pulsated between her legs. And despite the horror of Serosen's poetic words, Selena found she wanted to run her hand along his massive, silken length, and wrap her lips around the bulging tip of his cock.

Selena shook her head, hair brushing her shoulders and back. *What in God's name is wrong with me? I'm in some strange fantasy world, and all I can think of is fucking a dark elf-man, and wanting more of him every second. Despite the dangers. Despite the fact that I've almost died – twice.*

And what had he called me?

"Mi'Awen – *my inspiration, my spirit, my heart.*"

The enormity of Serosen's words struck Selena at her core. *And he can also read my mind.*

She stopped and turned. Her eyes found his, patiently, intently, fastened on her. There was no deception in his gaze. No subversion or pride. It was the simple, open look of someone who cared deeply for another.

Even though Selena had grown up without her parents, there had been no lack of love in her spinster aunt's Phoenix household. Selena knew that look. She'd been cherished to the very end of her *tia's* life.

The urge to battle her dark prince fled like August rain in the desert. Surely nothing lasted for an eternity. Maybe the saying was merely a formality of his kind.

That had to be it.

She looked down at her arms and felt a strange fluttering in her belly. Selena quickly decided that she'd deal with the eternity aspect of things later. For now she'd play along until she could figure out exactly what the rules were in this new world.

She'd done very well back in Phoenix figuring out how to work the system to her advantage. In school without a mom or dad, she'd dealt with the normal questions and ridicule by out arguing or muscling anyone who dared try to manipulate or abuse her. People were quick to discover that size and stature were irrelevant to determination and authority when it came to Selena DeLaPava.

After taking a deep breath, Selena pushed hair behind her ears and began to walk in the general direction Serosen had been leading them until…

She rubbed a hand across her lips and forced the image from her mind, of his tongue darting between her teeth. *Stay focused, Selena. Don't give in to carnal urges. Not until you know better what you're dealing with.*

Relief surged through her when Serosen fell into step beside her, leaving enough space between them to keep their bodies from accidentally touching one another.

"So," Selena started as their pace quickened with Serosen taking the lead. "What is this place called?"

"The dimension itself is *Tir na n-Og*. The lands in which we currently travel are Tuathan," he replied, a whispering of pride in his husky voice. "We travel to the Winter Kingdome, where we will seek sanctuary in my tribe's demesne."

A spark of memory teased Selena's thoughts. "I've heard those terms before, from my girlfriend, Gwen. They were in relation to her archaeological studies in the highlands, if I remember correctly." Selena grinned at the memory of her golden-haired friend's misty-eyed enthusiasm. "I have to admit I tend not to pay much attention to her once she starts yapping about ancient history. She'll go on forever if you let her."

Pain stabbed at Selena at the thought of the terrific worry Gwen must be going through over Selena's disappearance. *What does she think happened to me?*

"She will not be aware of your disappearance yet."

Selena gasped and swung around, landing a heavy punch on Serosen's shoulder. "Stay out of my head, damn it!"

She caught his quick smile before he rubbed his arm. "Forgive me, *mi'Awen*. It comes as natural to me as anger comes to you."

"Oh!" Selena opened her mouth then slammed it closed. "You're impossible! Where I come from people's thoughts are their own, got it?"

Serosen's expression turned serious, and he stopped walking. "Truly, I am sorry. I forget how very different our worlds are. I will make a concerted effort to not partake of your thoughts without invitation...but know this." His unblinking gaze captured hers, and Selena felt that tingling in her chest again, as well as in the flesh of her forearms. "Through our bonding we are connected on a soul-deep level. That cannot be undone, and as a consequence, there will be times when our thoughts will be as one, permission or no." He moved closer. "Do you understand?"

Selena stepped back and threw up her hands. "Hell no!"

*Yes you do*, came a small voice in the back of her mind. But it wasn't her dark prince's voice, it was her own. She ignored it, turning her head away from her lover's hawk-sharp gaze and starting forward once more. She would be unable to resist him if he touched her with those strong, skillful fingers. Selena groaned inwardly and swallowed a sudden need to tell Serosen how much she wanted him. How connected she felt to him, despite her sharp words and objections.

*None of it makes any sense*, Selena thought, fighting to regain her composure. *My being here. The fact that I'm standing next to the stunning, shadow-man of my childhood fantasies...*

A jolt shot through Selena. It hadn't occurred to her to examine the fact that the dusky-skinned, beautiful and unearthly creature that she recalled from her childhood imaginings could be — was — real. She glanced at Serosen out of the corner of her eye.

*He looks just like him. It has to be him.*

Whenever she'd been lonely or in some sort of danger, she would see her dark prince's image in her mind's eye. He had fully appeared to her after her first horrible day of school when she'd fled into the desert behind her aunt's home. The children had spent the entire day making fun of her long, fiery hair. Telling her it looked like someone scribbled on her hair using purple, orange and red markers. And of course, being the smallest, they'd thought she could be easily pushed around. Given the tiniest crayon nubs. The ugliest desk. The last place in line.

It had never occurred to the isolated six-year-old that she was different, or that others might not love her as fully and as unconditionally as her aunt. She was determined never to set foot in school again, but she knew her aunt would insist. Selena's solution had been to scribble her ultimatum on the back of a Sunday church bulletin.

*I wil never go to the scool agan. I will live off the desert sands like the coyote and fox unteel you agree to let me sta home.*

A perfect solution in the young Selena's mind.

Selena smirked at the memory and shook her head. So stupid and foolish. She'd been raised twenty miles from the sprawling metropolis, near the Superstition Mountains, and the lush but unforgiving desert had been a comfortable playground. Until that night. Somehow Selena had become disoriented without a bright summer moon to illuminate her landmarks, and she became hopelessly lost. She followed an arroyo for what ended up being miles from her home, tired, thirsty and scared.

Exhausted, Selena had collapsed into the fine sand of the wash, crying out for her aunt. Of course, there'd been no answer. At some point Selena figured she must have fallen asleep, which was when she first saw her dark prince. He came to her on the comforting late summer breeze. The heady scent of night-blooming nicotiana and desert sage surrounded her, and she opened her eyes to stare directly into his steel-gray gaze and strong-jawed visage.

He whispered to her and held out a dusky-skinned, powerfully-built arm. "No harm will come to you, Selena." She reached out her small hand and noticed how real his fingers had felt. How supple, how firm. She rose, and stared in awe at her panther-like protector. He knelt, her tiny hand gripped in his larger one. "The wind and fox will lead you back home. Follow them now, and do not stray from the path they lay."

Selena opened her mouth to demand that *he* take her home, but before she could utter a word, he was gone, and she was left standing alone in the sandy arroyo. No, not entirely alone. Shivers flooded Selena once again at the potency of the memory. In front of her had sat a beautiful, gray-striped fox kit. Selena rarely saw foxes, but she knew they inhabited the area. *Tia* Sophia always said to see one brought good fortune to the deserving and a warning of swift retribution for those less worthy.

Not one to ignore good advice, Selena had followed the kit all the way back to the edge of their property. Once she realized where she was, the bristly fox shimmied into the underbrush and was gone.

She'd found her aunt wringing her hands and weeping on the front stoop. Upon seeing Selena emerge from between the overgrown citrus and palo verde trees that crowded their lot, she'd cried out in Spanish and rushed over to wrap Selena in her arms so tight Selena feared her aunt would break her in half. But *Tia* Sophia's arms had never felt so good. So right.

"I wish I could see you now, *Tia,* ask you what I should do."

Selena started when she realized she'd spoken aloud. She glanced over at Serosen to see if he'd noticed, but he continued to stride forward, his gaze focused on a barely visible path before them. Every now and then his gaze traveled to the treetops, as if watching for invisible lurkers.

Selena was reassured and irritated all at the same time by Serosen's sudden lack of interest in her thoughts and words. Since he seemed preoccupied, she took a moment to study her dark prince. He was as she remembered, tall and lithe, but in a powerful, muscular fashion that reminded her of a jungle cat. His hair, so dark to be almost blue, hung straight to his broad shoulders, and she couldn't help but focus on his finely arched ears. She hadn't recalled those from her youthful visions, but then again, the dreams had always been brief, and it had been his eyes that captured her attention and interest.

Was it possible that he had indeed come to her at those times? Or had it been more like...what did Gwen call it? Precognitive dreams? Tension crept between Selena's eyes and she rubbed her temples with her thumbs.

It was hard to believe she'd ever said her life was an uncomplicated bore. Gwen had told her she'd probably live to eat those words. Fresh from graduation at ASU, Selena normally spent her days schlepping files and researching boring divorce cases at the law office for which she worked, and had been inclined to think she was simply paying her dues.

But it hadn't taken more than five months of grunt work for Selena to realize it wasn't so much paying her dues as it was her being unwilling to leave the sanctuary of her childhood and strike out on her own. Since her aunt's death the year before, Selena had felt adrift, directionless. There was a frightening void within her that she had no clue how to fill.

Everything lacked *purpose*...meaning.

And now?

She drew in a deep breath and could almost taste the tang of nutmeg, tree sap and rich loam from the forest surrounding her. There were other scents, too, complicated ones that Selena had no reference to draw upon to describe them. Sweet and dusty, mild and so potently organic, it was nearly intoxicating.

Well, her current situation was as far from boring as one could get. There was nothing "normal" or monotonous about it, either. And, Selena realized with some surprise, she no longer felt that void. Nor did she feel directionless. She knew exactly where she was going. What had Serosen said? To the Winter Kingdome, wherever that was. To the sanctuary of *his* family.

The thought of meeting his family left Selena weak in the knees. What would they be like? Would they all be as tall, beautiful and intimidating as Serosen?

Selena lifted her head. Visually, the world in which they traveled was just as impressive as its aroma. The forest was thick with cinnamon, ash and white-barked trees. Some rose so high, Selena could only guess at their height. The leaves of all the trees were in full autumn glory, from bright crimson, to pumpkin orange and various shades of yellow. And as they traveled, foliage drifted to the ground in a steady rain of vivid color. Where they now walked, only the slightest hint of a dark path could be seen. The rest of the forest floor was dotted with the occasional clump of ochre-colored grass, struggling for sun beneath the dense canopy.

"Serosen," Selena said, knowing their silence had been compatible, but needing to put some of the pieces of her current situation to rights. "My familiarity with Celtic legend is murky at best. What exactly *are* you? I thought most elves were, well, you know, all fair and golden like"

She'd almost said "the golden god." It was funny, but compared to Serosen, the blond elf didn't seem attractive at all, but rather tawdry and cheap, like a boozed up Vegas stripper. All show and no substance.

"Like Du'an?" he asked, a dangerous glint in his eye.

"Well, uh, yes, actually." Selena pushed hair behind her ear. "At least that's how our movies and popular fiction portray them."

Serosen smiled grimly as his eyes scanned the forest around them. "Your Terran history is flawed, at best, strangled and suppressed at its worst." He breathed deep, his eyes taking on a far away look. "There are many races of the Tuatha De Danann, some light, some dark, some stranger still, to a Terran eye."

His gaze touched on her, and Selena felt a tingling in her chest.

"My tribe is that of the Night Elves. We are as comfortable in the blackness of night as most are in the brightness of day. But it is not simply the color of our skin that bears the origin of our name."

He paused, and Selena studied her dark prince. It wasn't pride in his voice, or stature. It was a surety, a level of deeper wisdom that left Selena feeling safe—if still uninformed.

"Okay, well in most of the references I've come across in our literature, Dark Elves were, for lack of a better term, evil. Obviously another fallacy," commented Selena, her fingers itching to trace the delicious outline of Serosen's bulging bicep as it swung beside her.

"Your legends are based on some fact, Selena, but there were those who feared true knowledge remaining with the people." A muscle twitched in his cheek, and Selena had to resist an urge to touch him—soothe him. "So they altered and buried much of the accurate accounts of your ancient ancestors and worldmates."

Selena felt a tightening in her chest. "You-you mean that once our worlds..." She waved a hand. "This one and mine, were combined? Elves actually lurked in the woods, faeries lived under hills and trolls squatted under bridges?"

Deep laughter shattered the stillness, and a trill of pleasure blossomed in Selena at the sound of it, rich and earthy. She frowned inwardly at her seeming inability to *not* feel an overwhelming urge to throw herself upon him whenever he spoke. Or moved. Or breathed. "What's so funny? I *told* you I'm not up on this stuff."

"Forgive me, *mi'Awen*. I cannot help be amused by the way you...phrase things." As he raised his arched brows and cleared his throat, Selena gave him a narrow-eyed look for good measure. "To some degree, yes, all those creatures you mentioned inhabited your Terran world and *Tir na n-Og*, but that was before the Great Separation."

Selena moved to keep pace with him as he spoke, her curiosity piqued. "Tell me about that. The Great Separation."

"A great battle arose in an attempt to suppress the dark forces that were desecrating both worlds. Humans and fey fought side by side to drive them back, but it wasn't enough."

Serosen's pace faltered, and Selena could see the tension flood his body. He took a deep breath, then released it before continuing. "The dark forces were strong then, fed by a bleak sense of desperation and brutality that raged throughout the lands."

A shiver edged its way up from Selena's abdomen and into her forearms. She rubbed them, trying to quell a deep sense of unease. "So, there was a great fiery clash. And they were obviously driven back, otherwise my world and yours would be a pit of hellish creatures and terror. So where did the separation angle come in?"

Serosen gazed at her sharply, and Selena wondered what she'd said to garner such a look. It softened, and for a moment, she wondered if she'd seen it at all. "Actually, we were losing until…" He paused. "Until help arrived from powerful allies." Serosen pushed thick, feathery ferns out of their way, the trail growing more congested with encroaching forest. "As a result, barriers both natural, and later, elf-wrought, were formed between our worlds. Barriers that could only be breeched by trained and trusted gatekeepers—on both sides. And that is how it has been for well over three thousand Terran years."

A thought occurred to Selena and with a hand to her chest, she blurted out, "You're not—are *you* over three thousand years old?"

Serosen's teeth flashed white in the shadowed forest glade. "Alas, no. I was not even a spark of prethought to my grandsere and mere during the Great War. I am just over five-hundred Terran years. Of course, time moves differently in *Tir na n-Og*."

"Just what *is* that difference? You said Gwen would not realize I was gone yet."

"We will move through a full moon cycle before an hour has passed in your world," Serosen said as his long legs continued to swallow up the path before them.

Selena did some quick calculations as she rushed to keep up. "So, we age quicker here? I thought it was just the opposite. All our legends talk about the land of Fey as being some type of eternal kingdom of youth."

A sudden lifting of her hair startled Selena and she raised her arm, knocking Serosen's hand away. She caught his quick smile, before his expression went back to one of patient amusement. "Our time is not linear as it appears to be on your world, and it affects the residents here differently. For example, your hair…" He motioned to her head, this time not touching, and Selena ran her own hand through her wild locks.

"What about it?" she challenged. She had forever been teased about her hair. The color, strange. The texture, thick yet silky, and with a complete mind of its own when it came to being tamed in a braid or ponytail.

"Do you notice anything different?" Serosen asked.

Selena pulled her hair around to the front, and her eyes widened as the tresses fell nearly to her waist. "Ohmygod. They—it's grown almost a foot and a half!"

"In this world, all things flesh and elemental rebuild and repair themselves with great swiftness. So while you could indeed live an entire Terran lifetime in *Tir na n-Og*, only a year shall pass in your world. I will not be considered old until I am well into my fifteen-hundredth year. And even then, I would have the choice of leaving my body behind and transcending to a higher plane, or remaining on *Tir na n-Og* in a physically limited, yet more spiritually expansive capacity."

Selena shook her head, knocking wayward leaves away from her face. It was all so much to take in! But somehow, it made sense. Which was even stranger. "So elves are not immortal, as our legends have it?"

He chuckled, and she gazed appreciatively at her dark prince. How she'd love to wrap her arms around his broad chest and press herself against his massive cock—

Digging in her heels, she barely managed to stop before bumping headfirst into Serosen who had halted in front of her. Facing her, he smiled, and Selena felt all resistance she pretended to have to his charismatic persona melt away like Italian ice on a hot day.

"Not in the sense your scholars and scribes dictate. There is birth, death and rebirth for all things, Selena." He lifted a hand, and around his fingertips fluttered an iridescent moth, its wings a mottled shade of blues, pinks and purples.

*Beautiful,* Selena thought, her eyes trailing the luminescent creature.

Serosen drew a circle in the air, and Selena could have sworn lights trailed from his fingertips. "From the most supreme beast to the tiniest insect. We are all a part of the great spiral of life." Colored circles of luminosity blinked to life before them. "Here life is extended due to the magickal properties of *Tir na n-Og* and its denizens, but our physical forms are not meant for forever. Of course, our spiritual beings are unquestionably eternal." His gaze shifted to Selena's face. "Is it not taught the same by your hierophants…er…priests?"

Priests. The word conjured up images of she and her aunt kneeling in prayer at St. Catherine's Cathedral. Selena had always loved the chanting and singsong voices in which the clergy spoke and intoned the rituals. The rich scent of the incense, the expansive yet intimate feel of the sanctuary. "Yes. It was much the same, but somehow...different," she finished, her eyes following the moth's trek as it fluttered inches from her nose passing through the glowing circle Serosen had drawn in the air. Her eyes crossed in an attempt to follow its hypnotic flight.

She laughed, and Serosen joined her with his own appealing chuckle. Selena's heart swelled. *Why does all of this feel so familiar, so right?*

Before she could think to answer her own question, she looked up to her dark prince standing directly in front of her, his steel-gray eyes glittering with an inner passion that robbed her breath.

He lifted a hand to her hair once more. His fingertips brushed her neck, sending pulses of electricity through her body. "So beautiful...from without..." He dipped his head, his lips, warm, caressed her temple. "And within."

Moisture flooded Selena's aching clit and desire curled deep inside her belly. She knew it was crazy to feel so turned on by a guy she'd just met—let alone a creature from another dimension, but there was no denying she wanted him like she'd never wanted anyone else in her entire life.

Selena placed both palms on Serosen's chest, marveling at the hardness beneath her hands. She traced his pecs up to his muscular neck, then on to his strong jaw. "Have you looked in a mirror, big guy?"

Standing on tiptoe, Selena pressed her lips to his, hesitantly at first, unsettled at the fact her body had simply taken over her good sense.

His lips were soft, yet there was strength even in the curve of the pliant flesh. And the taste of him, piquant and warm, like a long sip of spiced cider.

As her tongue teased the edges of his lips, Serosen gripped her ass and lifted her clear off the ground.

His strength—he carried her, effortless, like she was nothing more than a child. The power in his step as he strode forward, the feel of his iron hands holding her backside—incredible.

Selena's heart rate doubled. All the time he walked, Serosen kissed her, demanding more of her with his darting tongue.

Damn, but she wanted to give him more. She wanted to give him everything. Her body trembled with anticipation and an animal craving for her elfin lover.

## Chapter Eleven

*I must have her now.* Serosen pinned Selena against a smooth-barked ash. She felt so delicate, so perfect in his grasp.

*Mine. Mine forever.*

His thoughts whirled as he caressed her thighs and pushed himself fully against her, his cock grinding against her clothed slit. He knew it might be suicide to stop too long in one spot. To give Garethan's spies an opportunity to track them.

He heard her gasp, her hands twined in his hair, and Serosen's worries were buried under his throbbing need.

She wanted him. Maybe as much as he wanted her.

*Goddess, let it be so.*

"Woman, I will die now if I do not bury myself within your hot quim," he growled against her lips.

His bride giggled, and Serosen pulled back slightly, his brows raised. "You find that amusing?"

"I-I'm sorry. I've never heard that term before. Quim? Do you mean..." Serosen could tell she was having a hard time naming her woman's core, and he loved her even more for her innocence.

He grinned and nipped her bottom lip.

Goddess, but she was beautiful. Her brilliant eyes darkened with barely controlled anticipation as he brushed a kiss across her clothed puckered nipples. Seeing her flush with desire nearly drove him to complete madness.

A snarl tore loose from the depths of Serosen's throat, and in a fraction of a second he'd commanded both their garments to the forest floor, leaving them bare in the cool, shadowy woods. Surprise was evident on Selena's face.

Surprise — and more excitement.

Serosen pinned her with a hungry stare. His entire body screamed for him to throw Selena onto the carpet of autumn leaves and thrust into her quim until she begged for more — but no. 'Twould be a mistake to take liberties at this exceptional moment, when her heart was so close to accepting their bonding.

"Would you have me, then, Selena?" Serosen asked, his heart aching to hear a welcoming answer.

Selena nearly came just watching the elfin giant fight to control his lust.

*He wants me. He really, really wants me. Oh, my God. What have I gotten myself into?* Selena closed her mouth and raised her chin imperiously. "Well, I—I..." She shook her head. "Damn, I don't even know what to say."

Serosen grinned slyly. "Say nothing, *mi'Awen*. Speak with your body."

Selena heard a groan and realized it came from her own lips. No man had ever spoken to her like this. No man had ever claimed her so completely with a gaze, a sentence, an embrace.

*I'm about to screw an elf. A delectable, hunk of elf.* The realization was terrifying and outrageously erotic all at the same time. Tingles erupted from her abdomen to settle languidly into her most intimate places.

Selena found her courage and leaned forward until they were face to face. She touched her lips to his, and ran her tongue over his pearly teeth while feathering her fingers across the tips of his ears.

She was rewarded with a fervent growl as he nipped her bottom lip again.

"Show me how much you want me," she whispered, unnerved and highly aroused by her own daring.

With his hands holding her full ass, Serosen dropped to his knees and laid Selena gently on the soft ground. Selena allowed herself to sink into the fragrant leaves, feathery beneath her bare back, and surrender her body to his ardent gaze.

His sultry eyes roamed her nakedness, beginning at her feet and moving slowly up, resting appreciatively at the throbbing triangle of her pussy. Selena was half mad with want of his caress, his touch. But his eyes continued to roam. A muscle twitched in his jaw, and Selena started with the realization that he desired to touch her as much as she wanted him to.

*Why is he waiting? Why doesn't he take what he's already told me is his?*

Their eyes met, and Selena shivered with anticipation. He knelt between her legs, and with hands on either side of her body, he rubbed his magnificent chest against the tips of her breasts. Selena was breathless with want—need.

"Selena, *mi'Awen*, will you permit me to enter your body, your mind, your spirit?"

Shocked by his words, Selena could only stare at him incredulously as every inch of her skin screamed for his tongue, his fingers, his cock.

Still, he waited, his dark eyes caressing her where she lay.

"Yes, damn you!" Selena yelled breathlessly. "For God's sake, yes. I want you, Serosen. Every blessed piece of you. Please—"

Having apparently heard the magic words, Serosen shifted down her body until his handsome face was even with her pussy. With a satisfied smile, he delved into her dripping folds. Selena dug her fingers into the top of his head and gasped as he laved her clit as if he knew the map to the fire buried deep in her soul. Flames tore through her entire body, and elf or man, Selena could not imagine turning him away at that moment. Couldn't bear the thought of it.

*Not now. Not ever. Oh my God!*

"So ripe for my tongue, like the sweetest bearwood berry, juicy and red," he murmured against her slit, sending bolts of pleasure straight to her heart.

And then he stole into her mind again, whispering words of passion as he teased her clit with his long tongue, eliciting another round of "Ohmygods" Selena couldn't control.

This was better than imagination. Much better than dreams.

Serosen's own need skyrocketed at the look of rapture on his woman's face as her spread thighs trembled on either side of his head. Her fingers had migrated to her large, burgundy nipples, rolling and plucking each taut bud.

"Look at me, Selena," he commanded. "Watch me lick your sweet juices."

He wanted her to witness his worship of her womanness in all its stunning and delectable forms.

Her gaze lowered, her profound eyes midnight blue with passion.

Serosen plunged his tongue deep into her woman's core, and he felt both through their mind-link and physically, his bride's control shatter as her orgasm took her. Her scream drove the birds from the canopy, as Serosen lapped at her succulent slit until her tremors eased.

"Oh...I..." Selena reached down and pulled Serosen up by his hair. When their eyes were level, she said with all seriousness, "How did you *do* that?"

Serosen cupped her full breast, marveling at the silken beauty of the golden mounds. "With all sincerity, *mi'Awen*," he said, his heart filled with tenderness.

Selena's hand dropped to Serosen's rigid staff, and his breath caught in his throat as she ran her fingers along its length to massage the wetness at its tip. "So silken and smooth over such hardness," she murmured.

She continued to stroke, her hands cupping him from base to stem, and it took all of Serosen's control to not explode onto her belly and thighs. *So giving, my new bride. Even with her fears she opens herself to me.*

Her eyes lifted, and Serosen noted the glint of authority burning in their depths. "Stand up," she whispered. "I want to taste you...feel you at the back of my throat."

He traced a finger down his lover's cheek. "Selena, you do not have to—"

Her eyes spat fire. "Are you saying I'm not capable of pleasuring you like you did me? Stand up!"

He stood in one fluid motion, his body screaming with barely controlled desire. "Never would I think that, milady. I have every confidence that you—"

Her tongue flicked out to tease the pulsating head of his cock.

Serosen groaned and placed both his hands on the tree to keep from falling upon his soulmate and rutting like a seasoned stag. Up on her knees, she cupped his balls then leaned in. He watched as his fiery goddess smiled appreciatively before wrapping her pink lips around his shaft and taking his length all the way into her mouth. Serosen's body spasmed, every muscle tight as corded wood as his delicious bride sucked and pumped at his rigid cock.

Never had Serosen felt such pleasure, and he knew he was seconds away from coming in her sweet mouth, regardless of his supreme control. No woman, human or fey had ever brought him to such a precipice.

"*Mi'Awen*, if you do not stop I will—"

Selena gripped his buttocks and took his cock deeper into her mouth, her tongue whipping around his thrusting rod as she drove him faster. Serosen threw back his head and roared with the force of his orgasm, letting his juices shoot into his bride's adoring mouth. She swallowed and licked away every drop of his release, and Serosen felt his heart expand with more than simple affection for his beautiful, passionate and lustful soulmate.

*I love her.* There was no question that the fates had chosen wisely. *She is my heart. Now and forever.*

Still feeling the afterglow of his release, he reached down and eased Selena to her feet.

Her lips pink and swollen, she smiled at him playfully. "Did that please you, *milord*?" she asked.

Serosen felt his cock harden again, to near painful proportions.

"Let me show you how much it pleased me," he growled, lifting her so that her back was against the tree, his hands under her ass.

His finger slipped across her folds, then plunged into her channel. Selena gasped. "Please, I need you, Serosen…"

He flicked her clit. "You already have me, *mi'Awen*…" And with that his finger parted her folds and he rammed his rod into her tight channel.

Selena cried out and wrapped her legs around his hips, allowing him fuller access. Serosen groaned at his bride's tender surrender.

"Let me have all of you," Selena pleaded, her hands migrating to just above his hips and pulling him into her. Obliging, Serosen leaned in fully, then began driving his shaft to the hilt within Selena's hot sheath.

The inner heat of their *danu awen* began to build, and like their first mating, Serosen let it grow and consume them. Truth, he would have been powerless to stop it.

Selena reveled in the powerful fullness of his cock inside her. The pounding rhythm—the slick feel of their juices mingling. Within moments she felt the melding sensation build as it had the first time in the glade. A touch of fear wiggled into her mind—*What if I lose myself in him? What if our joined experience truly bonds our souls forever?*

Her lover's mind-touch filled her. *"We are not slaves to one another,* mi'Awen. *There is only power and beauty in the joining of our* danu awen.*"*

Like a silken caress his thoughts calmed and reassured her. Selena released her fear, and the magickal sensations of their joining erupted from within her heart outward, surging through every organ and extremity, to burst forth on waves of dual consciousness.

She rode the waves, experiencing her own rolling release as well as her lover's powerful orgasm. And even as their minds slipped apart, Selena felt a small part of herself lodge within her dark prince, somewhere near his heart, and she wondered if he was also within hers.

The thought was amazing and frightening, but she was much too sated to worry about it now.

As Serosen lowered them to the leaf-littered ground, their rapid heartbeats beat out a matching staccato rhythm. Selena curled into his chest, her hand stroking his jaw with cool fingers. "Is-is that the norm for sex in the land of fey?"

Serosen breathed deep of his bride's sage and orange blossom scent. "Only between soulmates, *mi'Awen*."

There was more he wasn't telling her. Selena sensed it like a monsoon storm breaking across the desert sky. She leaned up on her elbow and looked into his gorgeous eyes. "*And?*" she asked through elf-speak, allowing herself to play with her newfound abilities.

Serosen smiled and responded in kind. *"We are taught there is a heartmatch for each of us, one we can fully bond with for all eternity, but in truth, the youth of our tribes are more concerned with frivolous sex play than finding their soulmate."*

A sliver of doubt stabbed at Selena's heart. *"Then it doesn't happen for everyone? How can you be sure we were meant to be together, then?"*

He pulled her into his embrace. *"There is no doubt. I can feel it in the very depths of my soul. Can you not?"*

Through their heart connection, Selena was aware of the undercurrent of worry behind Serosen's words. She could not fathom hurting her dark prince by saying she wasn't certain, nor could she bear to lie.

Instead she changed the subject. "Soulmates. They don't talk about that in our traditional religious circles. That concept is left to new agers and love thumpers from the 70s."

Selena turned to see Serosen's puzzled expression.

"Having a hard time understanding, big guy?" She pinched the end of his nose, hoping her playful words would distract him from his earlier question. She wasn't ready to admit that she was bonded, heart and soul, to this dark elf for what constituted an eternity. "Now you know how it feels to be completely lost and bewildered. This place is beautiful, but quite dangerous, I think. Like you."

Serosen's expression instantly changed, and Selena felt the shift within him from attentive lover to worried protector. He smoothed hair away from her face and placed a kiss over her brow. "We must move on, *mi'Awen*."

Selena sighed. "I know."

He rose, lifting her up with him. In an instant, Serosen produced a supple cloth, and with expert hands, massaged and wiped her entire body clean. Selena had no doubt the material was something other than simple terry cloth, as it quickly erased all traces of their lovemaking, leaving her feeling fresh, her skin lightly scented with sandalwood and spice. He did the same for himself after handing Selena her clothes.

"We will be harder to track this way," Serosen murmured, staring at her with oh-so-obvious male appreciation.

Selena felt his eyes on her as she dressed. By his gaze, she could tell that he'd prefer she stay naked as a jaybird, and Selena couldn't resist teasing him by fumbling with the laces over her generous breasts, allowing a nipple to stray from its confines before she safely tucked everything away.

Selena felt deliciously wanton, and judging by the look of hunger on his splendid face, she knew she'd come very close to engaging a repeat performance of just moments before.

"Woman, you were sent to drive me out of my mind," Serosen growled as he gathered their things, his eyes never straying from her.

Red-faced and grinning, Selena fell into step beside her dark lover and shrugged. "Sorry. I don't know what came over me."

Without warning, Serosen wrapped her in his embrace and stole a ravaging kiss, one hand cupping her aching breast.

Selena groaned into his mouth, instant fire shooting through her abdomen and pussy.

Serosen released her lips but held her gaze. "You are mine, *mi'Awen*. I will destroy anyone who tries to separate us."

Selena's eyebrows rose, and her lips trembled. *Okay, what does that mean? Who's trying to separate us?*

But Serosen failed to respond to her inner dialogue.

She could taste a deep fear lurking in his heart, and the thought that she was the cause was more than she could bear.

With a hand on his arm she stood on tiptoe and placed a delicate kiss upon each cheek, then whispered in his ear. "I feel it too, my dark prince. There's magic between us. I just don't understand it. Give me time."

He pulled her into his arms once more, this time tenderly. He kissed the top of her head, then released her. "Come. The sooner we arrive at our sanctuary, the sooner we can spend hours learning each other's pleasures."

Selena grinned, a thrill shooting through her at the thought. "Lead on, big guy."

He held out a hand, and together they melted into the forest heading north.

## Chapter Twelve

While they trekked through the colorful woods, Selena could think of nothing but the powerful scenes of their lovemaking. Her nipples and pussy ached with the thought of her lover's skilled tongue and cock.

*God, how could anything feel so good?* Gwen's brother Curt was a nasty, flaccid slug compared to Serosen. No one had made her feel so full, so loved. As bizarre as the experience had been, Selena had no doubt that she and Serosen were indeed 'fated' to be together.

Not that Selena was ever one to listen to fate. She made her own fate. And maybe Serosen *would* prove to be the man, er, elf, she chose to spend the rest of her life with.

Then again, maybe not. She would be the one to decide. Not some ritual. Or bizarre circumstance.

With that firmly in mind, Selena allowed herself to become immersed in the sights, sounds, and scents as their pace quickened. Birds flitted high above their heads, and Selena caught only a glimpse of their brightly hued feathers. The sky peeked through in splashes of filtered light, and Selena found herself longing to see a vast expanse of blue and wide-open spaces.

While beautiful, the forest had begun to feel confining.

Serosen's voice eased into her mind like the gentlest of touches. *"Try to match my pace,* mi'Awen. *We must travel faster."*

Selena sensed a measure of worry and urgency behind her lover's words, and chills feathered across her neck. She knew they were running from something or someone — but what or who exactly? He'd never explained, and Selena found her mind filling in with all sorts of horrible possibilities…like the monsters that had attacked them earlier.

That was enough to get Selena moving. They changed from a brisk walk into a jog, and then into a steady run. The forest became a blur of color and scent. Selena didn't object to their pace, it simply became imperative that she match it. It seemed to Selena that Serosen's feet hardly touched the ground as he melted into the woods. Every now and then she felt Serosen's touch within her mind…not probing or intrusive, merely a gentle caress to ensure her level of comfort.

Selena found it odd that somehow she knew all of this without words, but it wasn't the time for questions. Her hair streamed behind her in a wake as her feet hummed over the uneven forest floor. Blood pumped through every extremity, but Selena realized she didn't feel fatigued or even winded as their sprint escalated.

A muted sensation of heat grew in Selena's abdomen, moving its way through her legs, then up to her arms and chest, blossoming at her neck and head. Her face felt hot, but it wasn't uncomfortable. She accepted the feeling and fed on it…drawing the richly scented woodland deep into her lungs. The cool air seemed to crackle within her, sending pings of fresh energy to her stressed muscles.

Her eyes fastened on Serosen's rippling back as he jetted around tree and bush, and smiling grimly, Selena followed. Her legs flashed through the foliage like butter, and Selena felt a distant part of herself standing in awe.

*This isn't normal...*her skeptical voice said, but that other, more knowing part of her was inordinately pleased. It was thrilling, the breeze slicing through her hair and caressing her face, the electric force zinging along every nerve and through each pumping muscle.

She laughed aloud, her voice echoing through the surrounding woodland. It was perfect. The power of it. The rightness of such an unnatural race. Her expanded vision allowed her to take in the forest through a widened view—seeing miles of trees, meadows and mountains. Rounded gray boulders jutted up into the darkening purple sky, and yes, there was Serosen, heading straight for them.

Selena gritted her teeth and demanded that her legs go faster. That her heart beat quicker, filling her extremities with much needed oxygen and vigor. And her body did as she demanded.

In moments she was directly behind Serosen, her gaze fixed on his flashing thighs and midnight hair. He was all she could suddenly see, and Selena's thoughts began to muddy. Visions of Serosen's taut body suspended above hers filled her mind's eye. His enormous, rock-hard cock pressed against her abdomen, and his mouth fastened on her nipples, sucking, teasing...

A groan built in her chest as she tried to shake herself free of the tempting image. Her legs suddenly grew weary, and her breath came in ragged gasps. She brought her attention back to Serosen and realized with shock that he wasn't slowing or switching direction to go around the massive boulders.

*Ohmygod.* Selena watched in horror and fascination as her dark prince ran directly *into* the great gray rocks...and disappeared.

Selena tried desperately to stop. Arms flailing, legs tangling in rust-colored vegetation as she cried out in dismay, "Serosen!" seconds before she struck the unforgiving boulders—face first. Pain, instant and sharp struck all her senses at once—then darkness.

\* \* \* \* \*

Serosen realized his error the moment he passed into the rock, but it was imperative he retain his focus and come to a halt within a channel before turning back. With a burst of speed, he broke through the skin of the granite behemoth into one of the many caves that permeated its interior. Once inside, Serosen turned and gathered the energies of the ancient rock into himself before pushing back into his spirit run.

Within a fraction of a second Serosen had cleared the rock and stood outside his entry point, dusk and dark clouds fast filling the sky. *Godsdamn*, thought Serosen as he knelt next to his unconscious bride, his heart thudding in fear for Selena's safety. He gently slipped his hand under her limp shoulders and brushed hair away from her face. After a quick examination, Serosen determined with relief that she was largely unhurt, except for a nasty lump on her forehead. The rest of her body had simply shut down from sheer exhaustion.

Cursing his foolishness, he lifted Selena and carried her to an ancient willow at the edge of the *Kaolen* forest. He and Vigil had sheltered within the willow on a previous occasion when they'd been forced to wait out a vicious gale brought on by a shunned kelpie.

He approached the great willow and asked permission of the wood sprite he knew resided there before ducking into the sheltered hollow. They would need to camp for at least part of the night, as Serosen detected a storm drifting in from the north. Every moment they spent fixed to one spot provided Garethan greater opportunity to locate them, but it couldn't be helped.

Serosen laid out his cloak and placed Selena upon it, and after getting permission from the sprite, started a low fire. The rich, hickory smoke traveled up the massive hollow trunk in a narrow wisp, exiting through a vent somewhere among its upper branches.

A sharp breeze whipped though the valley, and Serosen stiffened. He gazed out into the fast-darkening sky and clenched his jaw. There was more riding the storm than simple rain clouds. The breeze was laced with a bloody, metallic taint.

*Unsellie magick.*

Serosen looked at his bride and felt his heart clench. Swift fury filled him, and he wove a protection spell to fill the mouth of the willow, shielding the interior from the storm, as well as cloaking their *danu awen* from prying fingers of magick.

Garethan.

*You thought you could send Balor to claim her, sorcerer? You lost her then, and you shall not have her now.* Serosen dampened his thoughts, lest he draw the sorcerer even closer. He gathered his energies and bound them tight, then he gazed down at his soulmate. With some surprise, he realized that Selena's unique energies were already subdued, as if cloaking themselves without his intercession.

A niggling of unease was back to plague him, but perhaps, Serosen reasoned, Selena's mishap was a blessing in disguise. It had occurred to him as they traversed the barely discernable unicorn path that with their bonding and Eristta's gift of the enchanted garments, Selena might well be able to travel with spirit swiftness, if at a subdued pace. Which was better than them continuing on with no magickal intervention. Serosen wasn't above throwing Selena over his shoulder once more, but knew his prickly bride might be violently opposed to that method of travel.

So he'd invited her to follow him, and set a gradual pace. And she'd matched it.

Serosen looked down at his sleeping bride and felt that sense of otherness again. It was as if he were missing something that should be obvious. He brushed a hand down the side of her soft cheek, his chest aching with the extreme sense of connection he felt towards the Terran.

*Who is she?*

No ordinary Terran could have continued to match the increased level of enchanted flight that he'd set.

Near the end of their journey, Serosen had been flush with amazement at how well Selena's body had adjusted to the stress of the travel, easily sustaining the challenging pace—a skill that had taken him over a hundred years of training to master. He'd felt her thrill and sense of power at the accomplishment.

And then he'd spotted the *Colo'nai* mountain range. Could she maintain her concentration and trust enough to follow him through the granite face to the other side? There had been only one way to find out, and Serosen had decided to risk it. If she were able to accomplish the feat, there would be no doubt that his new bride was more than she seemed. And if that were the case, extra precautions would need to be taken, as well as a deeper investigation of her origins—*before* they arrived at the Winter Kingdome.

And if she could not…well, Serosen knew his sister's enchanted garments would prevent any serious harm from befalling her.

Serosen lay beside Selena, his arm draped protectively across her waist, her head tucked into the curve of his neck.

The warm sage and orange blossom scent of her skin filled his senses, and he sighed. As Serosen listened to the wind howl outside their modest sanctuary, his thoughts lingered on the necessity of solving the mystery of his bride's otherness before he asked his family to protect her with their lives. Which they would do regardless, but Serosen was unwilling to burden them with more unknowns.

As he stared at the steady rise and fall of his beloved's chest, an overwhelming desire warred with a deep, animal dread at a thought he'd dare not entertain—until now.

*Could Selena possibly be a tool of the Unsellie?*

\* \* \* \* \*

*Death littered the rolling moors. Bodies lay smoldering upon the once beautiful hills, and the stench reached her even at the great heights in which she traveled. Nausea filled her at the understanding of her terrible culpability in the carnage below.*

*"It was necessary, Fair One," came a melodious male voice. The voice that belonged to her soulmate. Even with the truth of his words, sorrow filled her.*

*"Why must it always be so?" she whispered.*

*She felt rather than heard his sigh. It grazed her soul like an ember flung into the storm. "It is their nature, Anelees. As we were created to restore the balance, they were created to destroy it."*

*"But will it be enough, Carradeim?" she asked. "My time is approaching. It calls to me from my very bones. Soon I will be gone from this place, this time, and the People will be left to their own devices."*

*She felt, rather than heard her lover's howl of despair. He dipped his head and touched her* danu awen *with his own. An ethereal glow enveloped them, and for a brief moment, Anelees felt comforted, safe.*

*"It is enough, Anelees, that you have been true to your destiny. That you protected and nurtured without thought to your own happiness. No matter the magnitude of this single victory, it is enough."*

*Anelees felt a tremor of warning, but it was too late. Netting, broad and finely-meshed, fell upon her and Carradeim, tangling them hopelessly, and turning them into a plummeting sphere.*

"*No!*" Selena woke with a scream, her hands flailing at the netting that bound her. *I must free myself without using —*

"Selena!"

Her lover's sharp call brought Selena crashing out of her dream and into—

Selena blinked rapidly, her hands still gripping at invisible threads, her head spinning. "Where-where am I?" she choked out, her gaze trying to find purchase in the unfamiliar darkness.

A warm hand cupped the back of her neck, and a spark of bluish light illuminated the room. Her dark prince filled her vision, and Selena clung to him, her arms wrapping around his bare chest, her legs twining with his, her head pressed into the curve of his muscular neck.

"Serosen. I-I thought you'd disappeared. Left me." Selena hated the uncharacteristic whine in her voice. That tone that shouted "I'm needy!" But she couldn't seem to help herself. The images, feelings and sensations of the dream filled her mind.

*What did it mean?* It had felt so real…so *fresh*, not like a dream at all. The thought left her cold, *freezing* cold, and she curled even tighter against Serosen's warm, hard body.

"You are safe, *mi'Awen.*" He pulled her to his chest. "We are inside a welcoming willow, shielded from the storm…and other things."

With the faint blue glow, Selena could make out the rough, bark-brown walls, and spiraling darkness that led up to many tunnels above their heads. But she *did* feel safe. Comforted and protected. Like curling up to *Tia* Sophia used to make her feel.

Well, not quite.

Selena was instantly aware of Serosen's naked body pressed against hers, and wetness flooded her pussy. Memories of their sexual encounters sent a jolt through her. *How could sex be so…magical?*

Maybe it wouldn't be this time. Maybe it would just be hot, animal sex. Selena smiled against Serosen's neck. Nothing wrong with that, right?

Shifting slightly, Selena placed a hand on his smooth chest, tracing the symbols that twined across the one side. Her hand stopped at his nipple, and she leaned in for taste. The silken flesh hardened under her tongue, and Selena felt his sharp intake of breath. She grinned around the taut bud and swirled her tongue across its tip. She traced the symbols with her tongue over his rib cage, across the rippling firmness of his abs, to the curve of his hip.

*He is so gorgeous*, Selena reflected, his skin a unique shade of powered graphite and rich earth tones. She'd never seen a more perfect specimen of man, er, elf. Her lips itched to taste him, to wrap her tongue over his luscious cock and sample the salty flavor.

*"I can hear your thoughts, Selena. You are transmitting them like thunder."*

Selena started, then laughed. She answered him in elf-speak. *"Well, does the direction of my thoughts please you?"*

In answer, Serosen moved to his knees, palmed his phenomenally large erection and brought it near her chin while he stroked her hair. Wetness flooded her, and Selena lifted her head, then wrapped her lips around the bulging tip. It was so engorged, Selena could barely fit it within the hot recesses of her mouth, and she groaned around his cock, imagining it plunging in and out of her pussy.

But first things first. Selena lapped at his massive rod, wetting it to better slide her entire mouth over its length. Selena took him all the way in to the back of her throat, pumping her mouth up and down the length of him, her hands cupping his ass to drive him deeper.

Serosen moaned, his powerful legs and hips moving to meet her sucking demands.

"My sweet, you drive — me — beyond my endur — "

Selena twirled her tongue over the tip of his cock as she sucked, her hand sliding and squeezing from base to stem. Her nipples puckered almost painfully as she felt her lover so near to coming, and she increased her rhythm, demanding more, pumping his cock. *"Come in my mouth!"* she commanded her dark prince in elf-speak.

Serosen roared, his juices spurting into Selena's mouth as she milked him dry.

Selena didn't have a chance to lay her head on her lover's stomach and relish his sated state, as Serosen's hands fastened on her arms and lifted her. She straddled his prone body, her breasts suspended over his hungry mouth. Serosen wrapped his tongue around the large burgundy areola and nipped the pebble-hard tip. Selena gasped, the exquisite pleasure of his tongue bringing her oh-so-close to climax. He moved from one aching bud to the other, sucking, flicking and teasing until Selena thought she would scream.

He moved his fingers down and parted her folds, his hand rubbing her clit in slow, taunting spirals. "So hot and swollen for me, Selena. Tell me your luscious, hot slit is for my cock alone."

His finger thrust deep, and Selena moaned.

"Say it, Selena," he growled. "Say you are mine. Only mine." Again, he thrust and teased her clit.

*How can I say it?*

His finger continued to thrust and tease, and Selena knew she would lose her mind from the delicious feel of it. *Am I? Am I his, now and forever?*

"Say it, *mi'Awen*," he whispered, his mouth fastening once more on her aching burgundy tips.

Need unfurled deep in her belly, and Selena surrendered to the moment and her powerful dark elf. "I'm yours, Serosen. Yours alone to tease to madness. To fuck to near insanity!" Selena finished, back arched.

*Night Elves: Wicked Pleasures*

Large hands gripped her hips and lifted, impaling Selena upon his thick, rock-hard shaft. Selena gasped with the pure pleasure of his rod filling every space within her channel. The spicy male scent of him flooded her senses, and Selena wanted to drink all of him in—forever.

Their eyes locked, Selena straddling Serosen's taut, rippling body, her hair flowing around them in a fiery cloud.

"You shall never leave me, Selena. I would hunt you to the ends of all worlds."

A sharp sense of *déjà vu* pierced Selena at his words, but the feeling dissolved as Serosen began to slide his cock in and out of her pussy. His hands lifted and pulled her down in time with his thrusting hips, driving him ever deeper, until she could feel him at the gate to her womb.

"Yes!" Selena gasped, "I am yours, dark prince, as I always have been."

*Why am I saying this?* Her pleasure-fogged brain railed against the words, but they poured out of her, like some always-known but forgotten song.

Selena's body jerked with the force of her orgasm, lights dancing behind her eyes, as she relished the sense of being one with her mate.

*Mate? Mate! I've lost my mind.*

Serosen came with an animal bellow, holding Selena tight to his groin as he emptied his seed deep inside her, and Selena gloried in the mystical sensation of their spirits linking them inexplicably.

She fell onto Serosen's chest, her breath falling out in shortened gasps. She could feel his heartbeat strong and fast under her breast, and she kissed the skin above his heart.

Selena searched out her lover's arresting gaze, and felt her heart swell and shudder at the compassion and love she found there. Shocked, she realized she wanted nothing more but to wake up every morning to that gaze. To look at his gorgeous face and feel the hard contours of his body at each moment of the day.

She groaned and curled into Serosen's chest. "Ohmygod, as much as I hate to admit it, you're winning my heart, Serosen," she whispered. "And if you do, you'll be the first to possess it. Break it, and I'll rip you to bits."

She felt his chuckle, and his hand caressed the back of her neck. "I have no doubt of that, *mi'Awen*. But I have no intention of ever sundering our bond."

Confident of his sincerity, Selena allowed herself a moment of contentment, and tried not to think of her dream and the fact that someone, some *thing* was chasing them down in the hopes of doing who-knows-what.

In the comfortable aftermath of their lovemaking, Selena finally noticed the pounding rain assaulting their warm refuge. She gazed toward the narrow breach, and perceived the shimmer of silvery-blue that flowed across the opening. No water penetrated the hollow, and she realized Serosen had woven some type of magical barrier to keep the rain out.

As she reached out to stroke the twinkling air, a face materialized outside the cavity.

Selena reared back with a scream.

Serosen jumped into a defensive crouch, glittering black blade in hand. *"Move away from the doorway, Selena!"* came his warning growl.

She complied, then watched in astonishment as the face reappeared, an impish grin on its exotic, cat-like visage. A bright, ringing voice broke into her thoughts, *"Knock! Knock!"*

Serosen cursed colorfully, then stabbed the blade back into its holster next to his boots before crossing the small space to the entry. With a wave of his hand he dissolved the barrier and pulled the creature inside, the mystical doorway reinstating itself the instant she entered. "Godsdamn, Eristta." Serosen's annoyance punctuated each word. "I nearly blasted you to Balor!"

# Chapter Thirteen

*She's gorgeous*, was Selena's first thought.

The sinuous creature's pearly teeth flashed in the gloom as she embraced Serosen, then planted a wet one on his handsome cheek.

Displeasure sparked in Selena's gut, and she bit her tongue to keep from demanding the skinny wench get her perfect little hands off her man.

"It's good to see you too, brother."

Brother!

Of course. His sister, Eristta, the one who had made her clothes — which was when Selena remembered she wasn't wearing any. She bent and yanked the cloak up to hide her curves.

Neither of them seemed to notice her embarrassment.

Serosen looked as if he wanted to shake and hug Eristta at the same time. "Eristta, it isn't possible that you found me on your own." He held her at arm's length, his look fierce. "Nor can I fathom why you would even try such a foolish thing!"

Ignoring him, Eristta broke free, midnight hair so like her brother's swishing around slender shoulders.

Out of her damp locks flew a raucous pinprick of sizzling orange light.

Directly at Selena's face.

She cried out and held up her arms.

*"Arock nar!"*

With Eristta's firm command, the tumbling ball of liquid light stopped on a dime. It hovered directly in front of Selena's face. She blinked once, twice, finally realizing she was looking at a perfect, miniature, naked little man—with wings. And pear-colored skin...that glowed.

Tinkerbell.

Damn if it wasn't Tinkerbell with... Yes. Selena couldn't resist looking. Tinkerbell with a tiny little prick.

Eristta burst out laughing, and the creature crossed its arms and gave a bark of outrage.

Selena looked at Serosen. *"Is he dangerous?"* she asked in elf-speak. *"Like those brownie things?"*

Before Serosen could answer, Eristta came up to Selena, her large, slightly slanted violet eyes shining. *"You have the ability to elf-speak,"* she said in pleasurable surprise. *"I had wondered if bonding with a Terran would generate that result."*

"Forget her astonishing abilities!" cried the creature, his voice quite masculine, despite his size. "She's insulted me! I demand penance!"

Eristta waved a hand at him, never taking her eyes off of Selena. "Put a cork in it, Darous." She reached out a faintly glowing, dusky-skinned hand and caressed a strand of Selena's hair. "Beautiful." Her eyes traveled over her from head to toe, and Selena gripped the cloak tighter, butterflies flitting through her abdomen.

Without warning Selena found herself buried in Eristta's embrace. The scent of lilacs and moonlight filled her senses. "Sister, how I have longed to meet you." Selena could feel Eristta's svelte body through the thin piece of cloth between them. Her pert breasts pressed tight against

Selena's own generous bosom, and a strange twist of desire zagged through her.

*What's wrong with me? I don't make it habit of finding other women attractive, and certainly not the sister of the guy I've been sleeping with!*

Serosen's sibling released her long enough to plant a warm kiss upon each of Selena's cheeks, then gave her an intimate, knowing smile.

*Damn!* Selena blushed crimson. *I've got to learn to stop broadcasting my thoughts like a concert announcer.*

Eristta laughed, the sound ringing with delight. "Sit, sit!" She pulled Selena down next to her onto the earthen floor. "I didn't want to interrupt, but the storm was getting more, er, grasping, and I didn't want to make my presence known by lurking outside like a nasty troll."

She patted the ground on the other side. "Come, Serosen, we have much to discuss, and I have need of you to introduce your bride properly."

Serosen sighed and joined them on the floor, keeping an ever-watchful eye on the doorway. "Eristta, this is no time for formalities. Tell me how you found us."

Eristta rolled her eyes. "It's not as if we're going anywhere for some time, brother. And you are well acquainted with the fact that I'm not one to keep with formalities. I just need to know what to call this delicious creature you have taken as part of your soul."

Selena blushed, and circumspectly observed the dynamics between brother and sister. It was obvious that they were close, and despite Serosen's irritation, Selena could sense his deep respect and love for his sibling. It tingled within her own heart as if *she* were the one who'd been raised with Eristta. Helped her climb her first ash tree. Spell her first boggart.

*Where did that come from?*

The images had sprung unbidden and fully formed in her mind.

Selena rubbed her temple. The sensation was beyond odd, but Selena knew she couldn't get too hung up on semantics, otherwise she'd cease to function at all.

Serosen's steel-gray gaze darkened, and Selena knew he was close to losing it. He reached out and took his sister's hand. "Eristta, this is no game." His eyes flicked to Selena's face, and a tingle of unease flared in her breast. "I must know by what means you tracked us, and if you were followed."

The stunning elf leapt to her feet, eyes blazing. "Do you *dare* accuse me of games? After all I've seen. After our- our mother's..." She stopped and turned, her shoulders rising and falling rapidly with the force of her emotions.

Selena stood, empathy flooding her for this dark and lovely woman. She placed a hand on Eristta's shoulder. "I'm sure that's not what Serosen meant. He's just very uptight about..." Selena frowned and turned to Serosen. "I've been meaning to ask, exactly what *are* we running from? And why?"

Orange light zipped between her and her dark prince, stopping a hairsbreadth away. "From wickedness! Pure, unbridled evil, that's what!" Warm air buffeted Selena's cheeks from his rapidly fluttering gossamer wings.

"And evil's chasing us because?" Selena asked, hands in the air.

The creature's pinprick eyes glowed a brilliant amber. "She's not too bright, is she?" he said, looking at Eristta.

Selena poked a finger at the rude little man. "Listen up, whatever-you-are. I've had just about enough of crude little creatures, and I'm likely to lose my temper very quickly under the circumstances."

His almond eyes went wide. "Well! Rude too, I'd say!" With that he flitted back to Eristta and buried himself within her shining tresses.

Eristta smiled wryly and fluffed her hair. "You'll have to forgive Darous, he's a bit testy after all we went through to get here."

Serosen looked pointedly at his sister. "Which brings me back to my original question. How did you find Selena and me?"

"Ah, Selena. A beautiful name, and together your names ring of the same sustaining power, don't you think?"

Serosen raised his brows, his look severe.

Erissta sighed, her expression resigned. "Right. Well, I suppose I knew I couldn't avoid telling you forever."

Selena listened with rapt attention as Serosen's sister told a tale of shocking intrigue and audacity. Being held in seclusion with the other Night Elfin women, Eristta received word of his and Selena's bonding. It was then that she had enchanted the garments and sent them with Red Claw, only to receive word hours later that Garethan had finally broken his silence and had asked to speak with the High Council in preparation of a truce.

Eristta paced. "Well, it was obviously a ploy!" She stopped in front of Serosen. "And yet there were those who are willing to jeopardize their lives and our Kingdome to hear him out." She grabbed her brother's hands. "I had to find you. And it was not an easy task with those two watchdogs you have set upon me. In fact, I would not have found you at all if it were not for Darous and his excellent passion-sense."

Eristta released Serosen and turned to smile at Selena. "Darous can sense energies stimulated by great passion. Those who are bonded generate powerful fields, and it was through that we were able to track you." She looked back to her brother. "Thank the Goddess you two were more interested in each other than actually traveling or hiding, lest we never would have found you!"

Selena blushed crimson, but Serosen smiled softly before his expression sobered. "But if Darous was able to track us, then so may others." His gaze flicked to the darkened entrance. "We must leave as soon as this accursed storm lifts."

Sitting on her heels now, Eristta hugged herself. "We need you to put a stop to this insanity, Serosen. Peartoth and Culdhun are pushing Father to allow them to attend the gathering, and he is…considering it," she finished, as if the very words left a foul taste in her mouth. "Everyone seems to have lost their ability to see reason, and there is talk that because you have bonded with a Terran, that your influence is no longer a vital link in the eternal knot that binds the Winter Kingdome." She stared at Selena, her eyes darkening to almost black. "That somehow Garethan is responsible for bringing Selena here with the express purpose of rendering you impotent in the coming battle."

Selena gasped at Eristta's words, her stomach dropping into her toes. Serosen took his sister's hand, a muscle twitching ever-so-slightly along his jaw. "Eristta, you cannot believe—"

"Look," Selena said quietly, standing, her chest feeling as though it were being squeezed in a vice. "I don't want to come between you and your fam—"

Serosen raised a hand to cut her off. "You are not."

But he didn't sound certain.

Fingers of ice pricked Selena's heart. *Does he think that maybe I* am *merely a tool?*

*Am I?*

Dizziness swept through Selena and she sat—hard, her throat frozen.

Eristta knelt beside her and placed a warm hand on Selena's arm. "No, sister. I do not believe you to be a tool of Garethan. Not by choice…" Her violet gaze fastened on Serosen. "In any event."

Selena shook off Eristta's hand. "Okay, I've let too many things go without demanding answers." She fixed her lover with a firm glare. "*Now* I'm demanding. Why do *you* think I'm here?"

Before he could answer, a violent boom shook the willow, throwing all three of its denizens to the mossy floor.

The firewhit shot out of Eristta's hair, flaming blade in hand. "We have been found!" he called. "We must flee!"

"Who's found us?" Selena called as another loud boom sent splinters raining down upon their heads. Her heart thudded wildly.

Darous zipped through the air above Selena. "The Unsellie Wizard, you ignorant woman!"

Selena felt blood drain from her face at his words, and she looked first to Serosen, then Eristta.

Both of their expressions and bodies were frozen—unmoving.

Panic raced through Selena. She crawled to her dark prince. "Serosen!" she yelled directly into his face.

No answer.

She shook him, but his body remained stiff and unresponsive, his steel-gray gaze fixed upon nothing. Selena's gaze whipped to Eristta. She was the same as her brother, her violet eyes empty.

Dread robbed Selena of breath.

*What can I do?*

Cold seeped from the very walls of the willow, infecting Selena. She could *feel* him—the sorcerer.

"OhGod, OhGod," Selena murmured, her bare body erupting in goosebumps, as a sickening terror settled in her gut.

On hands and knees, she scrabbled to find anything to awaken Serosen. To bring back his powerful, reassuring presence.

Another blast. This one rending a tear in the trunk overhead.

An ear-piercing shriek filled the space around them, and Selena clapped her hands over her ears. A wooden, but very much female face materialized from the skin of the tree, her mouth unleashing another painful cry.

*The wood nymph.*

Selena wasn't certain how she knew this, but she did. And whatever was trying to get at them was killing the willow's benefactor to do it.

She gazed upward. Water sluiced through the small tear in the willow's skin, splashing upon the floor like dripping blood.

Yet another blow bashed the tree and Selena felt and heard roots snap free of their earthly moorings. Pain sliced through her heart as if it were her own body being ripped asunder.

She screamed right along with the wood nymph, hands clutching her sides.

The firewhit Darous spiraled in front of her and stopped, his radiance shocking her out of her stupor. "Use your own power, girl!" he shouted, his wings buzzing so fast Selena could scarce see him. "Drive him back so we may escape!"

Selena rounded on the little man, terror punctuating her words. "I don't have any power, you obnoxious little twit! I'm human!"

Darous flew closer, his amber eyes appraising her narrowly. His hands went to his naked hips. "Like centaur shit, you are," he said, his expression one of bewildered astonishment, then certainty. "There's power in you. And it definitely is *not* human in origin."

Selena was shocked into silence. "That's not true," she whispered, but even so, an odd warming sensation began filling her chest, growing, expanding. Out from her heart and into her abdomen it flowed. Slipping through her veins like liquid fire.

*What's happening to me?* Selena thought, her spine straightening, her entire body feeling as if it were elongating, flowing into more than what it was moments before.

Vaguely, she heard Darous gasp before the sensations superseded all thought and will. She closed her eyes and breathed deep, letting the sizzling vibrations zoom through her extremities. A languid sense of power — strength, seeped into her spirit, and she welcomed it. The energy amassed at the top of her skull searching for an egress from the confines of her body.

Dimly she heard a tiny voice at her ear — shouting — something. "Wait! Mistress, do not shift! Do not—"

White-hot light burned behind her eyes. Unable to contain it, Selena raised her face to the heavens, opened her eyes and shrieked.

An explosion of flame erased all thought, except one. *I am on fire. I am fire.*

A force left her body in one massive torrent. There was no pain. There was only the burning rush of uncontrollable energy.

Selena's entire consciousness seemed to be quickening out on that stream, and as she gasped for air, a distant part of her realized that she was losing herself, draining away — changing — in the wild mass of energy spiraling upward.

A desperate voice quickened into her thoughts. "Close your eyes, Mistress. For the love of your soulmate, shutter the window to your true self!"

*Serosen.*

A memory of a touch. The recollection of a kiss.

Selena recoiled, frantically fighting to stem the fiery surge.

But the force did not *want* to be suppressed. The power, Selena realized, was an intrinsic part of her, yet, not her. Beyond her. Ageless. Perpetual.

And she had chosen to unleash it.

Again.

Ripped from the present, Selena's awareness was flung to the earlier reality of her dream…

*"No!" she screeched, struggling for freedom. Refusing to contemplate doing what she knew would dissolve the netting and free her.*

*"Do it, Anelees," her soulmate whispered. Their eyes met, deep violet to emerald green. "Do not let them use me against you. Save yourself and our people."*

*Their spirits touched, but there was no soothing the horrific ache within her.*

*Carradeim spoke, "We shall meet on the other side, Fair One. Do what you know you must to leave this world in peace for a time."*

*Anelees gasped as she felt her heartmate pour his* danu awen *into her being, leaving him but a lifeless husk entwined with her larger, fast-falling form.*

*Grief splintered her.*

*A shriek fractured the countryside, causing people and animals to shield their ears and gape skyward.*

*Her thoughts turned inward, her resolve iron-clad as she allowed her energy to build.*

*They had gambled that she would not sacrifice her soulmate to free herself — suppressed like a wet blanket over a flame.*

*They'd been right about her, but had underestimated Carradeim's fierce love for his soulmate, his people, and his land.*

*"I will do this for the People," Anelees whispered as she continued to plummet, her words so soft they were as thistle down upon the wind, "and for you, my love."*

*Energy, swift and deadly, unfurled from within her, roiling outward on a wave of endless flame, scorching everything within her site. The netting fell to dust. The creatures responsible were incinerated and scattered upon the wind. Her soulmate's ashes swirled into thermals, which would spread them over the land he cherished above life.*

*And yet, she did not stop there. She continued to feed the power with her grief and pain. Until it grew completely beyond her, a massive, writhing ball of white-hot flame.*

*Her burning gaze fell upon the countryside, searching out the still beating heart of the evil that had besieged the people and land. She found it. A throbbing canker upon the back of their good earth.*

*Anelees knew her time had come to bring an end to the wickedness. Yet she knew their conclusion would also be hers.*

*Death called. Release beckoned. And as she speared toward her final destination, Anelees vowed it would not be in vain.*

*Speaking the language of the ancients, she placed a boon upon the seed of life within her, and wove that boon into the threads of fate.*

*Her spirit words reached even the furthest of ancient creatures, alerting them of her conscious deed. "Even though she must hold the power, my daughter shall also have the power of choice. To accept or to pass her heritage to another. Mark these words and remember them well!"*

*With that the flame became her and she it. Raining down upon the corruption of a millennia, and bringing it trembling to its knees.*

Selena screeched, feeling as though her body and spirit were being ripped in two. Fighting the wild energy and images of a past she knew intimately yet not at all, she forced her eyelids closed, cutting off the torrent of flames.

And with it her consciousness.

Blackness claimed her.

## Chapter Fourteen

Serosen knew only that he had been locked within himself as surely if someone had thrown him inside a dank cell and spelled the door closed for an eternity.

A distant part of him could sense Garethan's foul presence. Felt him battering at the gates of the willow's protective shield.

Ripping it asunder.

But he could not see it. Could not sense his soulmate's terror, or his sister's bright energy. He fought, but it was in vain, as he had no purchase from which to launch an attack. No ability, even, to marshal his own strength.

And then there was an explosion of light and heat that sent him spinning within his own form. He awoke just as his body struck the wall of the willow. Pain lanced through his back, stealing his breath.

But he was on his feet in an instant. His head whipped around the chamber, and blade in hand, he searched for his soulmate.

*Selena.*

She lay in a heap near the middle of the hollow. Serosen crossed to her side and knelt. Steam rose from Selena's inert form, and her hair lay in tangled spirals across her bare body.

"*Mi'Awen*," Serosen elf-spoke, brushing her spirit gently with his own. He determined with his mind caress that she was unharmed. Just deeply asleep, her body drained of energy.

*Thank the Goddess.* Serosen brushed hair away from her pale face, his chest aching with the thought that he could have lost her. And he, so easily incapacitated.

None other than Garethan could have launched such an attack.

He slipped a hand beneath Selena's neck and legs, lifting her to his chest and standing. It was then that Serosen felt the breeze upon his cheek and looked up. His gaze met clear, midnight sky. Stars filled the heavens, shining brightly down into their roofless hollow.

The top half of the willow had been blown away. Blackened tendrils of wood sent up small ribbons of smoke as tiny rivulets of water dripped into the hollow. Entire branches had been incinerated.

Serosen tore his eyes away and searched for his sister, praying she had survived.

He found her standing outside the willow. She shook her head and brushed at her clothes, before raising her face to meet his gaze through the hole in the tree she'd been blown through.

"Serosen," Eristta whispered, striding through the gaping wound to stand at her brother's side. "Selena. Is she…?"

"She is fine, as far as I can determine." Serosen closed his eyes and mind-searched for any indication of Garethan or his minion's presence.

There was none.

A niggling of wrongness settled in his chest. Where had Garethan gone? *And why?*

"Darous!"

Serosen turned at his sister's cry. She knelt and came back up cradling the tiny firewhit upon her palm. Her eyes were wide with fear for the creature she'd called friend from the time she was a babe in her nested cradle.

Eristta blew on his inert form. "Come, Darous, I know you are not so easily done away with."

"His wings." Serosen stared at the firewhit. "They are *singed*." Every bit of hair had been burned away from the tiny man, leaving his skin pink, like fresh-roasted duck, instead of its usual pear green.

He remained unmoving, and Eristta gazed at Serosen, tears swimming in her violet eyes. "What spelled flame could have done this to a firewhit?"

A cough. "Not what, who," came a raspy voice.

"Darous!" Eristta cried.

The firewhit sat up unsteadily, his eyes bloodshot. He touched a trembling hand to his pinkened face. After another series of coughs, he fought to stand, then decided against it.

"Faerie tits," he murmured, his butt plopping back onto Eristta's palm.

Eristta gently mind-kissed her long-time friend. *"Who did this, Darous? And more importantly, where are they now?"*

His amber gaze fell on Selena in Serosen's arms. "It is not for me to tell," he said softly, wrapping his torn and singed wings around his shoulders and chest.

Eristta's brows lifted in surprise. "What? Since when has Darous the all-knowing failed to tell a tale?"

Darous sighed, his expression somber. "Since now. I am sorry, Eristta. But I cannot say."

Serosen fixed Darous with a narrow gaze. "We need to know so that we may protect ourselves. This is—"

"Not a game! Yes, yes." Darous glared at Serosen, then motioned to his decrepit wings. "Do you think I do not know this, Elf?"

Serosen bit back a curt response. It was obvious that Darous understood the seriousness of the matter, and Serosen could not fathom why the firewhit would hold back.

Unless he'd been bound not to.

He met his sister's gaze and knew she'd drawn the same conclusion. Serosen inclined his head to Darous. "My apologies, firewhit." He turned, then laid Selena gently upon his cloak. "We make for the Winter Kingdome with all haste."

"I will keep watch while you dress and gather your supplies, brother," Eristta said, striding out of the blasted willow with Darous tucked safely between her breasts—a safe, warm spot to lick his wounds.

Serosen quickly clothed himself and Selena, then exited the willow with his soulmate in his arms. His spirit ached at the destruction of the tree. He'd searched for the sprite's presence, but had been unable to locate her. *"I am sorry,"* he said in elf-speak, hoping the wood nymph had not perished along with her charge.

"Serosen!"

He loped to Eristta's side.

Her violet eyes were shot through with silver as she focused on the woods to the north. "They come," she whispered.

Serosen could smell them without benefit of mind-travel.

*Golems.*

They were in no position to stand and fight.

It was time to flee.

\* \* \* \* \*

They ran the entire night, Serosen carrying Selena tight to his chest. By daybreak, the siblings crossed the southern border of the Autumn Kingdome into the land of the Night Elves.

Serosen stared at the distant, snow-capped vistas and sighed. Blessed cold stung Serosen's face, and he raised his gaze to the ice-blue sky, breathing deep of the energy laden air.

"Good to be home, eh, brother?" Eristta smiled, her pearly teeth shining.

"Yes," Serosen replied, tightening his hold on his bride, and wishing she were awake to take in her first view of the lands that were to be hers as much as they were his. His mind was rife with images of the many places and ways they would enjoy the pleasures of each other's bodies.

Atop Whitecliff's sheer towers. Beneath the enchanted ice caverns of Raven's Loch. In the bondmates pleasure room at the very heart of the palace.

He ran a finger across Selena's pale cheek, stopping at her succulent lips. How he missed their warm, citrus flavor and passionate depths.

"Serosen?"

He came back to the present with Eristta waving a long-fingered hand in front of his face. She pushed back the hood of her cloak and smiled softly. "There will be plenty of time for that frolic." Her expression sobered.

"After we solve the mystery of your bride and find a way to suppress Garethan—if at least for a time."

Serosen sighed and tucked a strand of fiery hair that they had trimmed to a manageable length into the fur-lined hood that Eristta had given Selena before they departed the willow. "Let us be as swift as the wind, then."

The siblings had taken no more than three steps when a powerful pounding shook the ground and brought them to a halt. Serosen tossed Selena over his shoulder and freed his fighting arm and blade. His sister followed suit, a kriss dagger quick to hand.

Back to back they faced the fast approaching riders.

Black, bark-brown and silver elfin steeds circled the pair, their riders heavily armed as if to war. Serosen recognized only a few of the Night Elf faces. Others were unfamiliar and base-looking.

*Mercenaries.*

Serosen's blood ran cold, then just as quickly, fire simmered beneath his calm exterior.

*Damned if Mercs are of my father's doing.*

"Lay down your arms, my lord," came Peartoth's deep rumble. "We wish you no harm."

Serosen stared at Peartoth's square-jawed visage. An aura of false authority had settled about his cousin, and a niggling of trepidation crept into Serosen's gut.

"By whose authority do you command the son of Alwyn Isil-Gan to lay down his trusted blade?" Serosen asked with deadly calm, his eyes sweeping the ensemble.

Peartoth and Culdhun exchanged guarded glances, before Peartoth shifted on his mount, the silver steed sidestepping with unease.

"We have news of your father, my lord. We have been patrolling the border in hopes of locating you…hence our swift arrival."

His eyes, along with everyone else's, flicked to Selena, and Serosen tightened his grip on his bride.

*It's not me they are looking to find. It is Selena.*

Anger seeped into Serosen like water to dry moss, but his sister's calming hand upon his arm stayed the fire that itched to be loosed from his palms.

He stepped closer. "What news have you of my father?"

Mahogany-haired Culdhun guided his steed forward, steam billowing from his mount's flaring nostrils. "He has taken ill, cousin. Even now he lies abed unable to issue orders. The elders have failed to divine the source of his ailment, and fear without you and your fine sister's influence, he will surely succumb."

Serosen smiled furtively as fingers of ice numbed his heart. "Where would you be with no reigning sovereign to issue decrees of defense and or attack?"

Peartoth cleared his throat. "Well, then, 'twould be up to the council to rule, my lord." He inclined his head. "Until such time as you could be sworn to the throne, of course. Which is how things have passed since moon change yesterday."

Eristta sheathed her dagger and motioned to riders at the edge of the throng. "Quickly, then! Lend us steeds so that we may fly to the palace without further delay!" Her voice rang with command, and after a pointed look from

Peartoth, two of the more unseemly mercenaries slipped silently to the ground and brought their mounts forward.

While her face was calm, Serosen sensed his sister's deep distress over the news of their father's illness, news that Serosen was not at all certain to be true. Something was afoot, and while he had a hard time entertaining the idea that his own blood could be party to a plot against his father, he understood the danger in trusting anyone save his closest friends and family.

Speaking of which...

"And Vigil?" Serosen asked as he swung both himself and Selena onto the ebony stallion in one seamless move. "He is to act as heir apparent if Eristta or I are unable to assume the throne. "

Culdhun flung hair from his narrow face and snorted. "Being absent in times of trouble seems to be an inherited trait." His silver eyes fastened on Serosen. "Your younger brother has been missing since moonrise two nights past. He brought word of your battle with the Golems, then melted into the forest and has not been heard from since, nor have the elders been able to scry his presence anywhere in *Tir na n-Og*." A muscle twitched in Culdhun's fox-like jaw. "How do you explain that, my lord?"

Serosen's steel-gray eyes flicked dismissively to his cousin. "I have no need to explain it, Culdhun."

Mind-linking with the steed, Serosen asked it to take them swiftly to Whitecliff. They turned as one. The equine's powerful legs propelled them forward until they were a blur streaking across the frozen earth of the Winter Kingdome.

\* \* \* \* \*

"My Lord!"

Serosen dismounted and strode under the arched amethyst lintel of Whitecliff and into the great hall before the footman could even complete his bow.

The hall stretched before him, light reflecting off its seamless windows, allowing a nearly 360-degree view of noble mountains, snow-draped valleys, crystal lochs and mysterious forests. Gems of various hues studded the winding obsidian staircase, and Serosen took them two at a time, Selena tight to his chest.

He felt Eristta close behind, and was grateful for her unyielding presence. Whatever was to come, Serosen knew he could count on Eristta to protect Selena if he were incapacitated.

Not that it would come to that.

Serosen's powerful stride ate up the curving aquamarine-floored hall as he headed for his father's rooms. The palace was curiously empty of servants and nobles. Since the Golems' attacks, it had become more a bastion of training and politicking than a blithe playground of bored Tuathan royalty, but there were still the salaried retainers. Not to mention the Night Rangers themselves.

Where were they?

The handful that had traveled with Culdhun and Peartoth were but a sliver of their forces, and the mercenaries looked to be of the Drow clan, a lawless band of elves that inhabited the abandoned dwarven caverns at Ethlinn on the boundary of the Winter and Autumn Kingdomes.

Not soldiers that any of the four Kingdomes would call upon unless the situation was indeed dire.

With a flick of his hand, he commanded the intricately carved double doors open, then walked through.

His gaze went instantly to the once luxurious four-poster bed at the center of the room. Normally the living wood of the bed twined with woody stems, hardy boles, and bloomed a profusion of white buds and bearberry clusters. Instead the bark was gray and lifeless, the stems withered and cracked, leaves dry and crumbled upon the slate floor.

"Father!" Eristta cried, rushing past Serosen to their father's bedside.

Gently Serosen laid Selena onto a plush chaise, kissed her forehead and wove a protection spell around her with a word, then went to join his sister.

"Eristta," Serosen said softly. She was prostrate across the body of a shriveled elf that had passed to the other side. Her hair splayed across his withered chest like obsidian against the palest of snow.

Serosen looked down at his father and grief, sharp and stupefying, lanced his heart. He did not need to search for Alwyn Isil-Gan's spirit. Serosen had known the moment he'd broken the seal on the door and entered the warded room that their father, their king, was gone.

This body was nothing more than wasting flesh, long dead. A cold fist of rage knotted in Serosen's gut. He knelt at his father's bedside and gripped the cold, papery hand. "I shall avenge thee, Father." Serosen stood and ran a hand down his sister's shining hair.

She raised her face, her violet eyes damp and dark with anguish. "Who has done this?" She waved a desperate hand. "And to leave him in this condition!

Where is Marta? Or Helliobore? And what of the elders? Surely they would not leave him to die alone…"

Eristta choked back a sob. Serosen placed a hand on her trembling arm. "Eristta, mark my words. This death is spellwrought. The entire room reeks of magick, yet it is not Unsellie in origin, which can mean only one thing."

He paused to allow her grief-stricken mind to awaken to his words. Her eyes widened. "No," she whispered. Eristta shook her head. "It cannot be."

"We have been betrayed, sister. Whitecliff is no longer ours."

His words were barely a whisper, and even as he said them, Serosen began drawing the energies from the mountain's frozen heart and its many denizens to hand. It was not a process of theft, but a call to lend their power temporarily to a finer purpose, and they responded in kind, filling Serosen with an outpouring of faith and hope.

Eristta stood and wiped tears from her face with the back of her hand, before drawing her dagger. "No longer ours? Surely that is not possible!"

"Cry no more, sister," came a resonant female voice.

Serosen and Eristta both turned to see Selena rise from the couch. Her hair flowed and twisted around her curvaceous body as if on an invisible wind. Serosen's heart lurched, and his groin pulsed with desire. And her skin…it glowed a mellow amber in the dim and desolate room. Her azure eyes brimmed with power and apprehension.

Serosen went to her side, but she held out a hand. "Please, don't touch me."

"Selena," Serosen whispered. *"Mi'Awen."* Serosen reached out to her in elf-speak.

She shook her head, hair bubbling around her like a fiery brook. "I don't want to hurt anyone else. I...back at the willow..." She bit her lower lip, her eyes downcast. *"What I did, Serosen."* Her eyes came up, and Serosen was struck by the desolation and power surging beneath the surface.

Fingers of trepidation curled in Serosen's gut and moved up to grip his heart.

The blasted willow. Darous's injuries.

*Selena's doing.*

It didn't seem possible—or even plausible, but as he stared at his unearthly bride, sensed her energy brimming with magick, olde magick, he knew it was true.

Perhaps a part of him had always known.

Oh-so-gently he reached out toward Selena with his mind-touch. He caressed her heart, her spirit. Her energies were still her own, but there was now—more.

Selena sighed, then sobbed at his touch, collapsing forward into his physical arms. "*Mi'Awen*," Serosen said as he clutched her to him, his hand running down her hair. "You may be more than human, but it does not change my love for you. Nor are you a danger to me." He tipped her tear-streaked face up to meet his eyes. "We are as one, remember?"

Selena shuddered, and buried her face into his chest. "Yes, yes, how could I ever forget that experience?" Her body shuddered. "But what am I?" she asked, her voice ringing through every nerve of his body. "I have had these...memories. Or dreams. I'm not sure what they are, only that they are somehow me, yet not me."

Eristta walked forward and placed a hand on Selena's back. "Sister. We will help you. You are not alone in this."

Selena raised her head and pulled back slightly to face Eristta. "Thank you," she said with all sincerity, and Serosen squeezed her to him once more, before releasing her.

His sister embraced Selena, and Selena hiccupped as the two gripped one another.

"Hey!" came a muffled voice. "I'd prefer not to die by breast suffocation!"

Eristta and Selena drew apart. Darous peeked out from between Eristta's modest cleavage, his pear skin still showing a slight blush.

Selena gasped, and reached to pluck the little man out. "Darous! You're alive!"

He crossed his arm and inclined his head. "Brilliant observation, mistress."

She inspected him carefully, and Serosen was relieved to notice that Darous's wings had already begun healing, the transparent tissue knitting itself together in various spots.

"I thought... I had assumed..."

Darous waved a hand. "Think nothing of it. I'd rather perish in the flames of antiquity than be captured and disintegrated by that foul sorcerer's tainted powers."

"Flames of antiquity?" Eristta said, eyebrows rising.

The firewhit sat up straighter. "A figure of speech," he murmured. His eyes traveled to the bed. "Oh my. Is that the king?"

Selena placed Darous back into the front of Eristta's bodice. "That is what I was trying to tell you," Selena said as she walked over to the bed, her skin glowing once more. She looked down on their father's inert form, her face strangely calm.

"You told me not to cry," Eristta said as she joined Selena at the bedside. "Why? My father...my only sire is"

Selena raised a hand to silence her. "No. No, you don't understand." She gazed at Serosen, and he felt her call to his heart. He joined her and Eristta. Selena motioned to the body. "This is not your father."

Eristta drew in a sharp breath and Serosen's eyes snapped to his bride. "What do you mean?"

"It's a..." Her brow creased in thought, then relaxed as the word came to her. "Simulacrum. A replication of his being formed from pieces of his essence."

Serosen was rocked by her explanation, and he and Eristta exchanged shocked glances. "But," Eristta started, "how could you know such a thing? I did not detect trickery. Nor can I sense my father's danu awen anywhere beyond this room."

"I have been unable to sense him as well," Serosen said, his chest tight.

Selena waved a hand over the body, and in an instant the corpse fell to ash.

Eristta gave a cry, and knelt as Serosen reached out to touch the pile of grit upon the bed. Not ash. *Dust*. Dirt. Earth.

His steel-gray gaze went appreciatively to Selena. "You are right." He stared into his bride's unearthly gaze. "The simulacrum was expertly done. Flawless. I've never seen the like."

"Nor I," whispered Eristta as she stood. "But how could you have known, and how did you break the spell?"

Selena looked at them both, her gaze filled with fear and awe. "I don't know. When I woke and saw the two of you standing over it, I just knew." Selena stared at her hands and turned them over. "And I don't know how I did that. Not here, and not back at the willow. It just...happens. It's like there is a part of me that takes over. A part that knows more than I can even imagine possible."

*There is something...a remembrance from my studies, perhaps?* Serosen felt a niggling of awareness, but it was just beyond his reach. Frustrated but relieved that his soulmate was awake and unharmed, he pulled Selena into his arms, and allowed himself a moment of peace as she melded into him, breast, hip and thigh.

"It matters not, *mi'Awen*," he whispered into her ear. "We will figure it out. We should just be thankful that you are able to do what you did. Otherwise we would have all been taken or destroyed by Garethan."

Selena brushed a hand across Serosen's jaw. "I can't explain where your father is, or why you can't sense him," she murmured. "I just know he's not dead."

A clanging from outside the doors drew the trio's attention. In poured Peartoth and his retinue of paid soldiers, all heavily armed. They filled the entryway and fanned out to cut off any exit. Calmly, Serosen released Selena and pushed her slightly behind him, with Eristta on the other side, the bed at their backs.

"I would name you traitor," Serosen said to Peartoth. "If naming you at all was of any importance." He fixed his cousin with a fierce look. "Where is my father?"

Peartoth's eyes flicked to the ashy lump on the bed, and Serosen detected a glimmer of surprise. Any pretense his cousin thought to sustain vanished, and the planes of his broad face hardened with hatred.

"We were assured that you would not be able to detect the simulacrum. Not that it matters." Peartoth's thick lips curled with malice, and Serosen felt Eristta stiffen with outrage beside him. She made to move forward, but Serosen held her back with a mind-touch.

*"Stay, sister,"* he elf-spoke. *"First we must discover who is behind Peartoth's sudden quest for advancement. There is no possibility that he spearheaded this insurgence on his own. For now we go along with whatever they propose — as long as we remain together. If not, we fight."* He made certain that Selena was privy to the entire exchange, and he felt her mind-touch of agreement. Serosen also felt the core of power lurking within his wife. He had no doubt Selena was more than capable of joining them in any fight, but at what cost?

The thought left him curiously proud and deeply apprehensive.

*We need time*, Serosen thought to himself, *to fathom Selena's true heritage and power.*

Peartoth stepped forward. "We are to take you to the throne room. Put down your weapons and come without a struggle, and there will be no bloodshed."

Serosen smiled furtively. "Yes, but ask yourself, Peartoth, whose blood would be spilled? Are you so certain it would be ours?"

His cousin shifted uncomfortably, and Serosen was more confident then ever that Peartoth and Culdhun were not the brains behind the insurrection. *The answer may indeed lie in the throne room.*

Without haste, Serosen laid his sword, then his dagger upon the floor. After a moment, Eristta did the same. Of course, Selena had no weapon to declare, other than what lay at her heart, and Serosen knew his cousin was wholly unaware of his bride's newfound abilities. They were very aware, though, of Serosen's powers, and it was with abundant caution that the soldiers ushered the trio from the room, down the hallway toward the throne room near the heart of the palace.

## Chapter Fifteen

Selena gazed upward as they traveled toward the throne room through vast and unrestricted archways of transparent citrine hue, unable to contain her astonishment. If there hadn't been swords at their backs, Selena would have stopped and oohed and ahhed at the perfect blending of natural elements with luxurious silks, velvets and soft lighting.

"This type of interior could make anyone look beautiful," she murmured under her breath, which earned her a surprised and amused look from Eristta.

Selena realized circumstances did not bode well for them, but more importantly, she recognized once and for all, that she was more than she had been hours and days before. Common sense told her that the catalyst had been her bonding with Serosen. Not that she'd change that for all the money in the world.

Or freedom.

She gazed at her dark lover and a thrill zagged through her abdomen. No. Whatever happened, she wouldn't trade a moment of her time with her dark prince. He had become everything to her. His presence alone gave her strength, purpose.

He had filled that void that existed within her since she before could remember. Serosen truly was her other half.

Her thoughts turned to that power that lurked inside and longed for acknowledgment—recognition.

Somehow she understood that she was still in control of it—if tenuously. When danger threatened it seemed to take over, which terrified and thrilled Selena all in the same breath.

Her biggest concern now was not hurting those she loved in the process of trying to protect them. The memory of the tremendous, wild energy that had erupted from her in the willow left her slightly nauseated as they crossed from the shining entryway, and into the cavernous throne room.

She felt Serosen stiffen beside her, and through their inner link, his swift and furious wave of emotion. "You!" he growled, sprinting forward with amazing speed.

He didn't get far. A retinue of soldiers blocked his path, but he swept them aside with a single blast of hot air conjured from a quick string of words and his upraised hands.

As Selena stood frozen, Eristta struggled against the hands of their captors. "You putrid troll spawn!" Eristta shrieked, her hair whipping violently in her struggles.

With Serosen only feet from the dais, Selena's eyes lifted to meet the clear green gaze of the golden god. He sat comfortably upon a massive, crystal throne, seemingly unconcerned with her soulmate's approach. "How lovely to see you again, my sweetling."

Her jaw dropped, and her heart quickened. "You," she whispered. "You are behind all of this?"

As Serosen made to stride up the steps, a surge of light and crack of what sounded like thunder drove him stumbling back. For the briefest of moments, ropes of color flashed across the surface of what must have been a shield that encircled the dais on which the golden god sat and two other brightly-robed figures stood.

*No, not a god.* Selena pulled herself up and narrowed her gaze. An elf. Serosen's cousin Du'an from the Summer Kingdome. She recalled the knowledge from her lover's memories. She knew with a gentle mind-touch that Serosen was unharmed by his contact with the shield. He stepped back, his hands in fists at his side. Selena noticed that no one tried to intercept him. They let him pace freely in front of Du'an, his eyes coursing with wrath.

"Du'an, surely you know I will kill you for this," Serosen said with all sincerity. His gaze flicked to the hooded figures flanking Du'an. "As well as your mages. They cannot protect you forever."

Without rising, Du'an chuckled and smoothed his luxurious golden locks away from his face. He glanced at the mages. "I'm certain you will try, cousin. And I am just as certain that you will not succeed." He leaned forward. "For you see, they are no ordinary mages."

The mages shifted, and as if operating from one mind, pushed their cowls back. Serosen and Eristta gasped and turned their heads. "Do not look upon their faces, Selena," Serosen shouted. He moved his body between her and the dais, his back to the mages.

Selena frowned, her view blocked by Serosen. Selena noticed that everyone else in the throne room had averted their eyes, and some of the stoic soldiers were nervously ringing a hand or rocking on their feet.

She stared at her dark prince. *"What are they? Why is everyone so fearful?"* she asked in elf-speak.

His face grim, Serosen answered, *"They are Death Mages. The darkest and most dire magickers of our kind. They never leave their sanctuary at the southern-most point of Tir na n-Og. That they would come here..."* His inner voice faded, and Selena felt her lover's deep shock and distress. *"I cannot imagine why they would agree to do such a thing. This at least explains the excellent simulacrum of Father and this blasted shield. They are consummate spellworkers."*

*"But why can't anyone look at them?"* Selena elf-spoke.

Serosen's lips tightened. *"To look upon their true face is certain death. They have amassed so much wild magick that their visual form exudes that fearsome energy. It is a countenance no creature, save a select and highly warded few, can look upon and live."*

"Come now, gentlemen." Du'an amused voice filled the room. "Our delicate guests and strapping soldiers seem highly unnerved by your visages. Please cover yourselves so we can once again resume our tête-à-tête."

The tension in the room perceptibly eased as the mages covered their faces, and eyes hesitantly rose once more.

Du'an stared at Serosen who had turned, then Eristta. "And as you can now see, it would be quite futile for either of you to set your hearts on resisting. Consequently, it's your lovely bride I'm here to...speak with. You and your beautiful sister are of little consequence at this juncture."

Selena felt Serosen's outrage, and heard Eristta's feral snarl. She also detected a fine, wild energy pulsating at her bond-sister's core. Somehow Selena knew that Eristta possessed a deep connection to the same power that pulsed in her own heart. The realization made her feel even more linked to Serosen and his bloodline. And protective. She was not about to allow either of them to be harmed. Not by Du'an. Not by any ugly-as-sin Death Mages.

Not a freakin' chance. Not after all they'd been through.

Selena stepped forward and her gaze fell upon Du'an. "I will come with you, Du'an, if you promise not to harm Serosen or Eristta."

Serosen's head whipped her direction. *"Selena. Do not speak your permission for such a thing. Here words have the power to bind—"*

Closing her eyes, Selena sent out fingers of reassurance to her elfin lover. *"Peace, love. Du'an will not harm me. And it's likely the only way we will discover who, or what, I am. And at this point, what choice do we really have?"*

She felt his resistance to her words and deep fear for her safety. *"Mi'Awen, if we fight, you may well be able to escape. Eristta and I can hold them back long enough for you to flee—"*

*"No!"* Selena shouted in elf-speak. *"You will not sacrifice yourselves for me. I will* not *allow it!"* Selena fought to contain the surge of emotion that threatened to undermine her resolve. With a concerted effort, she blocked Serosen's ardent protests from her mind, and refocused her attention on Du'an, purposely avoiding the robed figures at his side.

Selena walked forward unhindered until she was only inches away from the shield. "Listen up, Elf," she said. "I'll only make the offer once. Take too long accepting it, and all bets are off."

Selena allowed the barest hint of her power to surface. Her hair rose, flowing outward from her back and shoulders, and she felt that niggling of heat rise from her skin ever-so-subtly. An amber glow, not unlike the one that surrounded Darous, pulsated from her skin, and it took all Selena's attention to hold the power in check.

Du'an stood, his fluid grace marred by the abruptness of his movement. His golden-robed chest rose and fell with his rapid breath. "By the Goddess," he whispered. "I did not believe it."

He strolled down the dais until he stood only inches above Selena, the barrier of light glittering between them. "Cresen suspected Garethan's purpose in arranging for me to bring you here was borne from a deeper agenda than merely attempting to distract my commanding cousin." Du'an inspected her closely, as if examining some strange and fascinating insect. "But even with all his efforts to divine the source of Garethan's interest, all he could grasp was that you represented some sort of important token." His full lips twisted into a wicked grin. "After our little encounter, I assured him you were no more than a luscious piece of earth flesh meant for an elf's pleasure, but I can see now that I was indeed wrong."

Serosen was at her side, and Selena could feel the heat from his heart-fire combine with her own. It pulsated against the shield, sending off lances of rainbow-hued light. "Touch my wife and your death will not be a quick one, Du'an." Serosen spoke softly, but there was no missing the menace and deadly promise of his words.

Du'an's expression sobered. He looked at the motley ensemble and snapped his fingers. "Remove these prisoners to the Palivar Pens, where they shall remain..." His green gaze found Selena's azure one. "Unharmed, per the lady's instructions." Du'an looked at his cousin. "And if you are thinking of resisting as they remove you, think twice, cousins." He looked to the mages, who were doing something quick and snake-like with their hands.

Selena gasped and arched as a sharp pain lanced through her back. Her eyes searched for Serosen. Fear suffused his face.

"Stop!" he shouted as he held her.

Du'an grinned. "You see, if you resist, they will know, and your bride will suffer."

Selena sensed Serosen amassing his own power and wrapping it skillfully around his very soul. *"No,"* she whispered in elf-speak, her eyes never leaving her lover. *"Serosen, you must not fight. Not here. Not yet. Please, my love. Trust me in this. Somehow I know now is not the time."*

She sensed him hesitate, then withdraw his energies. Relief coursed through Selena, then just as quickly a fissure of dread. There was uncertainty buried behind her lover's smoky irises.

Eristta's words came back to her on a chill wind. *"...there is talk that because you have bonded with a Terran, that your influence is no longer a vital link in the eternal knot that binds the Winter Kingdome... That somehow Garethan is responsible for bringing Selena here with the express purpose of rendering you impotent in the coming battle."*

It was true. That's exactly what had happened. She *had* been a tool of the sorcerer. But not by choice. Nor was her decision to go with Du'an now a betrayal of Serosen and his sister. *How could he possibly think that?*

Hurt coursed through Selena, and she broke eye contact, her hand pressed to her chest. There was no time to debate or deny the accusation that hung silently in the air between them like thunderheads amassing before a violent storm. Serosen's and Eristta's safety was what mattered. Not their opinion of her.

Right?

Unable, or unwilling to answer her own question, Selena wiggled free of her lover's arms and turned to the mercenaries gathered behind them. "Take them away," she commanded, her eyes avoiding those of her lover as he was roughly pulled from her side.

She successfully blocked her mind to Serosen's words, unfortunately, she could not shield her ears from her bond-sister's shrieks. "Selena! I understand what you're trying to do, but it will not work! We must fight, sister! We must—"

Her cries were drowned out by Du'an's cutting laughter and the shuffling feet of soldiers as they escorted the siblings out of the throne room and to the pens to await God knew what.

Selena chewed her lower lip, her heart hammering. Earth, her old life, even her new life and her beautiful, sensitive lover suddenly seemed a million years away.

*What have I done?*

\* \* \* \* \*

"Brother, your silence worries me." Eristta's hands gripped the gilded bars that imprisoned them as she gazed out between the slats.

Serosen did not respond. His stare was fixed on the wide, empty space that encircled their spellwrought cage. There were no dungeons at Whitecliff. The pen that housed them had been carefully constructed by the Death Mages specifically to contain the energies and magick of the Isil-Gan bloodline. It sat in the center of one of the palace's many interlinked caverns in the bowels of the mountain on which Whitecliff was formed.

Thus confined, he and Eristta were impotent. Serosen was unable even to mind-link with Selena, nor pull the energies of the mountain to his aid. They were in effect cut off from anything and everything that might give them hope or succor.

*Damn that woman. What had she been thinking?*

"We should have fought," Serosen muttered, his heart near to breaking with the weight of concern it held for his bride.

"You know we could not, Ser. Not with the hold the mages had over Selena. They could have tortured her greatly..."

Serosen held up a hand to silence his sister, the images her words conjured near to cleaving his heart in two. And if Garethan decided to come... Serosen turned away, the thought too horrific to entertain. They still were not certain what Garethan was doing with all the Tuathan women he'd been abducting, and Serosen couldn't even fathom the purpose he had in store for Selena.

His beautiful, stubborn bride.

Eristta's cool hand alighted on his shoulder. "Brother, you realize she did what she did because she loves you, right?" A sigh. "She hoped to spare us."

Serosen slammed a fist into the bars, pain shooting up his arm. "But she has only delayed our deaths. I tried to explain, make her understand that our best chance at freedom had been to fight, but she blocked me out."

He faced his sister, his eyes feverish with hurt. "She blocked me out, Eristta. She should not have been able to do that, bonded as we are."

Eristta's gaze narrowed. "Are you thinking that perhaps your bonding was a deception? Some trick perpetuated by Garethan?" Her slender fingers moved to her throat.

The dark elf shook his head. "No." He raised his eyes, his expression hard. "I do not believe her deceptive. How can I after having tasted her soul?" He pressed a hand to his chest. "Felt her very heart. No. She is not in league with the sorcerer, but there is no doubt Garethan wants her—needs her for some purpose. To send Death Mages. What must he have promised them? The thought leaves me cold, Eristta."

Eristta laid her head upon her brother's shoulder. "Aye. Me too. Worried about so many things. Not the least of which, what has become of our brother and father, and all of our friends?"

They stood in silence for a moment, before Eristta smiled softly. Knowing that cunning grin, Serosen raised his eyebrows. "Is there something you want to tell me, Eristta?"

"Well, let's just say not all of our friends are missing or lost." She patted her bodice.

\* \* \* \* \*

Moments after Serosen and Eristta had been led away, the barrier fell, and Du'an completed his journey down the steps to stand before Selena on the throne room's polished floor. "Well now, it is just the two of us, my sweetling."

His smooth, honeyed voice flowed around Selena seductively, but she found no sway in his words. Not anymore. "If you're thinking you can re-enchant me, think again," she mumbled, her attention fixed on the heavily robed mages immobile on the podium.

She could feel Du'an's frown, and she couldn't help but smile. She turned to face him. "What, did you think I'd go falling all over you? Hike up my shirt and fondle my breasts in anticipation?"

His eyes widened, and he licked his lips hungrily.

Selena sighed in disgust and went back to studying the mages. "You're a joke, Du'an. An empty-headed pawn in whatever game Garethan is playing."

A hot hand gripped her arm, sending lances of pain up into her shoulder. "Do not get mouthy with me, *Terran*," Du'an spat. "I could easily snap your slender neck before you could blink a protest."

Selena met his tumultuous jade gaze. "Oh? I think not, elf." With only the tiniest level of intent, Selena raised the temperature of her skin, until Du'an yelped in pain and released her.

He stumbled back, holding his singed hand to his chest. "You-you burned me!"

"And there's more where that came from, you empty-headed dolt," came a diminutive murmur near Selena's ear.

*"Darous?"* Selena elf-spoke, her hand reaching to her hair.

*"Put your hand down, mistress! You do not want to alert them to my presence."*

Knowing instantly who Darous was alluding to, Selena flicked a glance at the mages and dropped her arm.

"Do not presume to touch me again," Selena said, trying to sound forceful. Inside she was overjoyed that she wasn't truly alone. She had felt a strange kinship with the firewhit since the incident at the willow. She couldn't explain it, but Darous felt like family—if albeit a disgruntled, puckish and slightly charred relation.

"Yes, Du'an. Please refrain from touching my charge."

Du'an and Selena turned as one, and Selena studied the man who strode into the chamber. He looked common enough, but from Du'an's pale face and the fact that he had instantly dropped to his knee in supplication, she figured the stranger wasn't as ordinary as he appeared.

A cool hiss in her ear set the hairs on the back of her neck on end. *"'Tis him! I cannot believe he has come."*

Selena tried not to visibly react to the firewhit's words. *"Are you saying this is, that this guy is—?"*

*"Garethan? Yes, yes!"* Darous cried in panicked elf-speak. *"Goddess save us."*

Selena felt him bury himself deep within her hair, and she suddenly wished she could hide as easily. There was nothing left to do but study the creature, or man, that everyone was so terrified of. He looked to be in his late thirties, of average height. Fit, but not stunningly built like her dark prince. Dressed in dark breeches, a loose, cream tunic and a simple brown cloak, the sorcerer was quite plain-looking. Even his face and demeanor was calm and seemingly regular. In fact, Selena realized as she considered his features, they were as ordinary as one could get. If not for the pointy ears, he'd simply pass for one of the crowd.

"And you are?" Selena asked as he neared, her heart up in her throat despite her observations.

He halted only a few feet away, then bowed, before straightening and gifting her with a smile that nearly stopped her heart.

*Oh, my,* Selena thought. *He's a different man altogether when he smiles.*

"It is a pleasure to finally make your acquaintance, Miss DeLaPava."

It took Selena a moment to respond. She had already begun to think herself far removed from that other life. That person. That name. "Well, ah…oh," Selena finally ended, her face burning.

*I'm acting like a love-struck fool!* Selena admonished herself, her thoughts tripping all over themselves.

*"That's what he's good at!"* Darous's voice blasted into her mind. *"Confusion. Deception. Don't let him fool you, mistress, he means you naught but ill!"*

Selena shook her head, trying to dislodge the haze that gripped her. It suddenly occurred to her to wonder when Darous had gone from calling her "girl" to "mistress?"

"I believe we have much to discuss," said Garethan, that winsome smile still shining on his abruptly handsome face. He held out a hand. "Come. We'll retire to a more private space."

Selena found herself staring at Garethan's outstretched hand. It was sun-browned and of regular muscle. And the nails—perfect. Neatly trimmed and buffed.

Like before, in the dark space where Selena had found herself held prisoner, she moved toward that hand. Within moments, she felt its touch upon her cheek, frighteningly cold and greasy, two things totally at odds with one another.

She tried to pull away, but it was as if she were glued to that palm. And a part of her longed to stay. To lose herself in the subtle sensations that were pricking at her consciousness.

Pleasure. Indulgence. Luxury.

The concepts whispered in her ear and traveled straight to the core of her physical self. She allowed her head to rest in the cup of his hand, her lips parted, eyes closed as the intoxicating sensations rolled through her.

"Yes, my love. I am the only source of power you will ever need or desire."

Selena knew she was losing herself. But she didn't care. His touch was an intimate caress of her soul. It was tantalizingly seductive. Both sexual, animal and intellectual, all in the same breath.

*"Mistress! Snap out of it!"*

The clang of the firewhit's voice sharp in her ear, followed by a flaring sting on her tender lobe, brought Selena's eyes snapping open.

"Ouch!" Selena cried, slapping a hand to her head.

Darous shot into the air, his wings beating out a frantic staccato rhythm. Upon seeing the firewhit, a sliver of Selena's senses returned, and she pulled away from the sorcerer just as his lips were descending. She stumbled backward, her head and face throbbing where he'd touched her.

The sorcerer's eyes flicked to Darous. "Damnable nuisance," he grunted, before making a pinching motion with his fingers. Darous screamed, the sound piercing Selena's soul.

"No!" Without thought, Selena reached to intercept the magick between Darous and Garethan. As her fingers closed around the force exiting Garethan, bright blue light arched off the tattoos that wound across her forearms.

Pain lanced through her hand, and she nearly collapsed with the intensity of it. She saw Darous fall to the floor through a fog of instant tears, but was unable to stop his plunge.

"Selena," Garethan coaxed, holding out his hand once more. The honeyed tenor of his voice commanded her. With her throbbing fingers pressed to her chest, Selena once again surged forward.

*"Look closer at his hand,"* a voice whispered in her thoughts.

She obeyed, and focused in on that simple, yet powerful hand. As she stared, waves seemed to shimmer and coalesce in the space around each digit. Narrowing her gaze, Selena detected a shift in her perception. The hand was still of ordinary structure and build, but it was no longer clean and tidy. His upturned palm was coated in red. Clots of dark blood ran in rivulets to drip off his wrist. And his fingers...dirt mixed with dried matter was crusted on, under and around his nails, giving his fingers a claw-like appearance.

Bloody palms. Muddy fingers.

*Dirty, dirty hands.* Hands that had commanded hundreds of deaths. Thousands of tortures. Countless crimes against the People of Fey.

*And the People of Earth.*

The knowledge burst fully-formed into her mind, and Selena sucked in a startled breath. The images of her dream—her memories. *The beating heart of the evil that besieged the People...*

Selena's suddenly un-ensorcelled gaze rose to meet Garethan's. His eyes were a soft brown, but at their core burned a dark, ageless iniquity. Eyes she recognized from another time. Another place.

A feeling of detachment surged through her, and she gave it full reign, understanding she was as yet an infant playing in a pool ten times bigger than her swimming skills allowed. As the sensation of duality took over, Selena retreated to the position of simple observer.

"We meet again," she heard herself say in an odd, resonant voice.

Garethan smiled and bowed once more. "Ah, Anelees. I wondered if a part of you yet thrived within your young charge."

Selena felt her eyebrows arch. "More than a part, Errabon. But that's neither here nor there. It is *her* time, after all, and I'll not ride her like a nagging toothache. Which means this situation must be resolved so she may have an opportunity to choose her destiny, whatever it may be."

The sorcerer looked thoughtful. He locked his hands behind his back. "Yes, I can see where you would want that, Anelees, having never been afforded that choice yourself. But that would not serve my plans at all." He fixed Selena and her internal boarder with a frozen, emotionless stare. "You cannot begrudge my superior skill that allowed detection of your charge unfettered in that wreck of a world you call abundant."

He smiled grimly, and Selena recoiled further within. *How had I ever thought him plain?* His face was no longer one of pleasant ambiguity, but rather deeply etched with wickedness.

Anelees sighed, and smoothed a hand over their fiery hair. "Yes. That you were able to do so was quite extraordinary." She glanced down at the still prostrating Du'an. "And that you were able to use *him* to do your dirty work? Even more remarkable."

Garethan smirked.

"But," Anelees said, "there are things you've likely overlooked in your self-gratifying haste."

The sorcerer didn't twitch a muscle at Anelees's words, but Selena sensed his indignation. "Oh? And pray tell what might those things be?"

Selena felt her lips stretch into a smile. "Well, I believe you are about to find out."

## Chapter Sixteen

Pacing, Serosen poured through the many lessons impressed upon him throughout his years of training—searching for anything that might win them their freedom. But there was nothing.

With a mumbled word, white flame lanced from his hand to explode ineffectively against the bars.

*I must get to Selena!* Muscles twitched in his jaw.

"Serosen."

He continued his three strides across and back, feeling like a caged panther.

"Serosen," came his sister's urgent whisper once more.

He turned to see Eristta staring off into the murky darkness beyond their prison.

She inclined her head, her violet eyes wide. "Do you see it?" she asked.

"What do you...?" Serosen stopped speaking. There. In one of the long tunnels that led off the main chamber, a pinprick of light. Then another. Several tiny *moving* sparkles.

Serosen gripped the bars, his heart thumping low and heavy. "I see it."

Eristta joined him, her gaze riveted. "I know that light pattern." She stared up at her brother. "But in all my days, I've never seen so many. Mere used to say there was a time when they traveled in a swarm. But after the Great Destruction, so many had been destroyed. The elders thought they would never recover in such numbers."

They watched in awe as the swirling, gyrating ball of light advanced. Soon they were coming not just from one tunnel, but from many, coalescing towards the cage that sat in the center of the great chamber.

"Firewhits," Serosen whispered.

Eristta laughed joyfully as the creatures burst into the main chamber. Millions of fiery bright amber bodies zipped and twirled around the cage, filling the cavern until the light from their flesh made it seem as if it were full noon on a hot summer day. Air from their fast moving wings buffeted the pair.

Serosen stared on in wonder. "Eristta, are they civilized? Can you speak to them?"

"I can try." She pressed her face to the bars. "Darous remembers nothing of his native folk, since he was rescued from a hungry Carrion bird and placed with me in the cradle for luck. I don't even know what language they speak!"

Eristta closed her eyes. The writhing ball of creatures surged forward, the luminosity bathing their bodies like a spotlight. At the head of the great swarm, hovered a single, tawny-hued firewhit female. Her kind eyes exuded a golden, sparkling glow, and her nude body was perfect in every aspect, if in miniature.

She zipped closer to Eristta's face, which was when Serosen noticed her smile. "We speak as well as thee, elfling. No need to use inner-speech," came a lilting voice. "I am Keelie'n."

Eristta opened her eyes, smiled and inclined her head. "Forgive me, bright one. I did not know."

The firewhit shrugged. "You cannot help your ignorance."

Serosen raised his eyebrows at this sister. Obviously, Darous's impertinence was not borne from Eristta spoiling him, it was genetic. "Lady," Serosen said, bowing at the waist. "We have need of your assistance." Serosen did not intend to waste any time in finding a way out of the cage. He had no doubt the sorcerer would soon arrive at Whitecliff. Selena had become too important of a pawn to leave her to Du'an's care. The thought made Serosen mad with the need for freedom.

The firewhit zoomed closer to Serosen, and he could feel the gentle heat rolling off her comely form. "Yes, Princeling. Do you think we traveled all this way and risked exposure simply to make your acquaintance?"

Annoyance mixed with amusement pricked at Serosen, but he kept his expression neutral. "Of course not, wise one, but time is of the essence. My bride has need of our aid, and I would go to her before she is ensorcelled by the evil one."

"The evil one?" Keelie'n screeched. Thousand of tiny voices chattered at once, making the chamber ring, and both siblings covered their ears.

Keelie'n waved the hive to silence then landed on Eristta's now open palm. "We had suspected his return, but we swore to stay sequestered until our mistress called." She sighed, her caramel hair lifting off her shoulders in wisps. "It has been so long…we were beginning to think perhaps she was lost to us forever. Trapped in the *Other World* where she was seeded."

*Seeded? Other World?* Awareness pulsed within Serosen. His mouth dry, he leaned down until he was level with the firewhit. "Your mistress...who is she?"

Keelie'n was silent, her eyes traveling from Eristta to Serosen and back. "Have so many forgotten her, then?" she whispered desolately. The firewhit rose off of Eristta's palm, her expression somber. "I did not believe it. But, I suppose I should not be surprised."

She whipped up into the massive throng before Serosen or Eristta could utter a word. The shining bodies drew together high above the cage, their light expanding akin to a pulsating sun.

Eristta gripped her brother's arm. "I don't know what they are doing, brother, but I do not think we are in any danger."

Serosen nodded. "No, but will they help us? Can they?"

In an instant, the writhing mass unraveled like a spinning thread, then formed a rippling arrow, which shot straight towards the cage. Eristta and Serosen stood their ground, hearts pounding, fists clenched.

As the bodies of light struck the prison, a great explosion rocked the chamber, knocking the siblings to the floor. Serosen was back up in the space of a heartbeat, and pulled Eristta up with him. The firewhits had rent the magick binding the cage, exposing a narrow fissure for the pair to escape. He shoved Eristta through the slit, then followed in her wake. The fiery bodies held it just until the siblings were through, before pouring out. The cage resealed itself with a resounding clap that shook the very mountain, and Serosen had no doubt the Death Mages would sense the penetration of their carefully wrought prison.

He turned to Keelie'n who had once again separated herself from the swarm. "Thank you. I am in your debt. If you ever have a need, you have but to call and I will come."

She inclined her tiny head, wings vibrating rapidly. "I do not think we are done helping each other this night, Princeling." She looked up and away, as if listening to an inner voice. "They are aware, now," she whispered.

Serosen knew who she meant, and dread settled in his gut. *Selena.* His eyes snapped to Eristta. "Come. We have a home to reclaim."

His sister's feline face hardened, her violet eyes glinting with silver sparks. "And you a bride to protect."

Elves and firewhits poured from the caverns and into the tunnels that led up to the palace like an unstoppable, shimmering ice flow.

\* \* \* \* \*

Garethan's eyes narrowed, and Selena could feel a palpable drop in the room's temperature. At the same time, the floor shuddered beneath their feet.

Selena felt rather than heard Anelees's gasp, and a ghastly tightening sensation gripped them. It was as if there was a horrendous weight on their chest, squeezing the breath right out of her. Selena managed to turn and stare wide-eyed as the cloaked Death Mages twisted their covered heads, and focused on the polished marble floor.

The figures hissed, and the sound reverberated through Selena like a rasp scraping against her soul.

*What are they doing?* Selena thought, reaching for the comforting presence of Anelees. She didn't answer. Instead Selena felt her benefactor retreating, her presence melting into the recesses of her mind. *No!* Selena shouted. *How can you leave me now?*

A warm, reassuring sensation brushed her heart. *"Peace, daughter. I would never abandon you, but this is your time. Your world to fight for — or not. I cannot interfere with your destiny. Truly, I should not have emerged at all, but I could not allow* him *to meddle until you had a better handle on exactly what you are fighting for."*

*What* am *I fighting for?* Selena thought, her entire form vibrating.

Anelees sighed. *"For a chance, daughter, at happiness."*

And she was gone. Selena extended herself, and found that wasn't entirely true. Her essence was still there, but not *her*.

*Snap out of it, Selena!*

Selena forced herself to take a deep breath, her lungs laboring. The Death Mages were still hissing, their bodies seemingly frozen in that half-bent position as they focused downward. Power wafted off of them in waves, and fear clutched at her heart.

*What the hell do I do now?* Sweat beaded between her breasts despite the sudden chill in the room. A hand brushed the back of her neck, and Selena spun. Trails of ice burned where Garethan touched her.

His brown eyes simmered with power. "Ah, your benefactor has abandoned you to your own devices." He nodded toward the mages. "And just in time, it appears, to spare herself the agony of watching a very distasteful scene."

Selena drew herself up and pushed her terror aside. "So, you intend to kill me? Is that why you came all this way? Made all these elaborate plans? Am I that much of a threat to you?"

Garethan laughed, his voice carrying through the great hall like a megaphone. "Ah, my dear. You were never a threat." He stepped forward, and Selena stepped back, her legs bumping into the dais steps.

*Trapped.* Selena looked wildly around, searching for an escape.

"My carefully laid plans will take time to bear through to fruition. Your presence is merely a catalyst from which to move those plans forward."

He drew a finger in the air and red spirals dissected the space between them. *I'm caught,* Selena realized, blood pounding in her ears. *Trapped between the sorcerer's magick and his nasty mages.*

As he continued to draw the strange symbols, Garethan also began to speak bizarre words. Ancient words.

Selena felt a gentle tugging — at first. Then a more insistent one, as he continued to chant and draw into the air. The swirling red symbols reached toward her, filling the space on either side like an upright column of crimson smoke.

*He's binding me*, Selena realized with shock. *Binding my powers!* The pulling was becoming an incessant yank at the very core of her being, and Selena gasped as vicious pain coursed through her abdomen.

*Fight him!* her mind screamed, but Selena was at a loss as to how. As the column encircled her, a foul stench of rotting meat mixed with overripe fruit filled her nostrils. She gagged, hands gripping her side.

"Do not fight it, Selena," came the sorcerer's calm voice. "In moments nothing will matter. There will be no more pain. No more fear or uncertainty."

Selena forced her gaze upward, her body shaking as if in the midst of a violent storm. Garethan's eyes were feverish with excitement and concentration as he continued to form the spell to bind her powers, and, Selena suspected, steal them. The sorcerer had never wanted her dead…he was too greedy. Needy.

No. He'd want more from her than simple death. He wanted what lay dormant at her core.

Panicked, Selena tried to retreat from the pain, and from what was happening outside her body. She dove inward, following the shining trail left by Anelees. *I must find that power! Hold onto it. Keep Garethan from pulling it from me.*

Selena wasn't certain she could do it, but she knew no other way. She couldn't fight the sorcerer physically. Not now that he'd worked the spell so succinctly around her pain-wracked body.

As she rushed to her core, Selena touched upon many different memories—energies within her. Flashes and pictures of other lives, strange creatures, vivid and powerful emotions coursed through her awareness. *I have lived many lives*, Selena realized. *Loved and lost many friends.*

Nearing her center, the memories became more intense, more chaotic in their structure and form, and Selena pulled away in horror.

*It's too overwhelming!* she screamed. *So much pain! Blood, and terror.*

*"Calm yourself, daughter."*

It was Anelees. Selena felt her warm hand upon her heart and Selena sobbed in relief.

*"Stand, Selena, and see me."*

Selena drew herself up, and with open eyes, stared at the woman whom she'd only felt as a presence within her mind. It was like looking into a mirror. Anelees smiled, and Selena realized that no, they were not identical. Anelees's hair, though quite similar, was brighter—more rust orange than deep burgundy. Her eyes were a deeper blue, nearly purple, and tipped up slightly at the ends. And her face...her face was much more fey.

*"Yes,"* Anelees said with a nod. *"We are one, yet individual."* She placed a hand to her heart, and Selena felt the touch upon her own breast. "It is here that we are the same."

Selena raised her hand to the same spot, and felt the thudding, natural rhythm of their lifeblood beating beneath her palm. "What are we?" she asked her benefactor.

Anelees inclined her regal head. *"To know that you must agree to go into your very heart, Selena. Into the core of your being, which as you realize, the creature whom you know as Garethan, is trying to forcibly remove. If he succeeds, and you are there when he does, you will be forever trapped within his own power until such time as he is destroyed."*

The mere thought left Selena breathless with dread. But after a moment, she looked Anelees straight in the eye. "Well, it's now or never, right? And if the bastard does manage to snag me, Serosen will blast him to fiery bits, freeing my soul to go about its business."

Laughter, full and joyful filled the space around them, and Selena returned Anelees's grin. *"Oh, daughter, you have a practicality I never had."* She motioned her graceful hand. *"Come, then. Let us see the story of your life, and reunite you with yourself."*

Selena gripped Anelees's hand, and they turned to face a towering wall of roaring flames. The warmth beat against Selena's face, but she was not burned. Quite the opposite, Selena felt a deep, urgent need to be within the flame. *To go home.*

And with that admission, they walked into the fiery glow.

The moment they stepped through, Selena was bombarded with the sensation of burning—but it was not painful. It was as if her very soul were afire, consumed yet reborn, all in the same breath, and Selena knew beyond a doubt that she was indeed home. *This* was what she was. Light. Knowledge. Flame and power.

Within her heart lay an ancient creature. One of antiquity. One that had been the protector of the People of Earth and the People of Fey from time immemorial.

Flames licked at Selena's spirit and flesh, gifting her with slivers of knowledge. Memories of other lives. Pieces of who they were and had been in a millennia of existences.

Selena understood that the ancient did not want her to feel besieged by her history. But there was something she had to know.

"How did I come to be a vessel of this power?" Selena asked. "How did I come to be who I am?"

Instantly Selena found herself in a position of observer as a great battle raged beneath her. Creatures, foul and evil, chopped and hacked at humans and fey alike on a blood-soaked battlefield. And at its heart, Selena sensed the terrifying core of evil that spurred them on.

*Garethan.*

Yet, not him. Something older, just as she was. She'd seen this scene before, in her dreams. A great call rent the air, and Selena watched in awe as a massive bird of flame dived from a roiling gray sky.

*Anelees.*

Her physical appearance was one of a flamewrought bird, its multihued plumage literally ablaze with power and deadly intent. But at its heart, Selena could see Anelees. Feel her pain. Her grief and unwavering determination to send Garethan—no, in this life, Errabon—back to his hell-dimension for another three thousand years.

Her dive took her directly into the heart of Errabon and his demon forces. Blinding white exploded, and a wave of power rolled across the earth. Selena shielded her spirit eyes.

And then it was over. From her point, Selena could see the separation between the worlds of fey and earth. The blast from Anelees left confusion and memory loss in its wake, and as the People of Earth forgot their magickal cousins, the People of Fey retreated to protect their way of life, and the boundaries between the two worlds were formed.

Time lapsed by in hundreds of years before Selena's gaze. The point of the blast on the great plain became buried under new growth and life.

And then after several thousand years, came a bright, gray striped fox. He coursed back and forth over the field for days, searching, sniffing, seeking—something. He lived on at the blast site, through seven summers, springs, autumns and winters. And finally, one spring day, the fox's ears pricked and his nose twitched and with wild abandon, he zeroed in on a spot in the field, and began to dig. Another six days the fox dug, hardly eating, hardly resting. And finally, he came up from a deep hole of his own making, with a large, obsidian black egg in his mouth.

Selena tracked the fox as he sprinted across the land of fey, passing between the newly formed Kingdomes, until he reached a gateway. It was, of course, guarded by an intimidating fair-skinned elf. But the fox was quick to trick the guardian into opening the portal just long enough for him to slip through unnoticed.

Following him through to the other side, Selena gasped as she recognized the vast, desert vistas and towering mountain range of the Superstitions, just outside of Phoenix.

Her home.

The fox scurried from the dark cave where he'd exited the portal, and started off across the sweltering desert sands. He ran, it seemed, with purpose, following some inner compass. He finally slowed when he came upon a lonely back road that cut through the desert. After a few moments, he stopped. Heat shimmered off the asphalt in waves.

Selena felt her heart knock up into her throat. Steaming upon the desolate roadway, sat two mangled cars that had collided at a crossroads. The fox sniffed, and Selena could taste the miasma of death that hung heavy in the air.

Without hesitation, the fox padded up to a Toyota, observed both adult occupants, their spirits already departed, then trotted into the blooming purple sage on the side of the roadway. Selena moved in closer, her entire form vibrating. There, wedged into the bush, sat a mangled blue car seat, and in it, a young infant, maybe three months old. She wasn't crying, despite the numerous cuts and bruises on her golden-skinned body. Her blue eyes alighted on the fox, and she reached out with both hands.

The fox stared at her for moment, before setting the black egg in her lap. He moved back and sat, his amber gaze fastened on the infant.

The child began to flail with her plump arms, and as her tiny fist landed on the egg, a loud *crack* filled the strangely quiet space. The egg separated, and out of the obsidian orb wafted a curl of sparkling ash. The infant drew the ash into her mouth, breathing it deep into her lungs, and Selena gasped suddenly, remembering that sensation—that moment when her entire life had changed—began anew.

Within seconds, the scrapes and bruises upon the child faded, and despite the blazing summer sun, she remained unburned and comfortable. The egg dissolved into dust, and for the next several hours, the fox sat beside his charge until another car stumbled upon the accident scene.

*"And that, daughter, is the story of your beginnings."*

Selena felt herself leave the scene of her past, and reform before Anelees in the fiery heart of her soul. Tears poured down Selena's cheeks, to drop into the void beneath her feet. "So, I am not merely a copy of you."

Anelees shook her head. *"No. Your human parents were the first ones to give you life. The Phoenix was the second. For without her intervention, you would have perished along that roadway. She always knows when it is time to be reborn, and what vessel has need of her – and she it."*

"So I was chosen," Selena said, finally beginning to understand.

*"Yes, and in essence, you chose her, as well. You had the option, even as that young soul, to move on into the afterlife, or take in the heart of the ancient that sought you."*

Anelees moved closer to Selena and placed her hand upon her shoulder. *"And you have yet another choice to make, daughter. For even though the Phoenix lives within you, you have yet to fully unleash her. To allow her to work through you to help protect the many creatures beneath her charge."*

Selena stared into Anelees's violet eyes. *"You.* You placed that boon upon us."

She nodded, her gaze somber. *"Yes. So very few of us, Selena, had ever been given an opportunity to realize we could choose to accept the power of the Phoenix, or pass it on to another. I wanted you to have that choice. So I charged the Phoenix to allow you that option when the time came, and she agreed."*

Warmth, acceptance and deep love filled Selena's soul, and Selena understood that the Phoenix did not begrudge her that choice.

"If I choose to accept the power, will I be doomed to the same fate as you, Anelees?" Selena asked, thinking of the horrible end of Anelees's soulmate, and her own ultimate sacrifice.

Anelees smiled sadly. *"I cannot say. Each of us must live our own fate. There was a time when the Phoenix existed in her raw state, but she could not sustain her sense of humanity, her connection with the very creatures she was charged to protect. So with the help of an ancient magician, the Phoenix began to reincarnate through physical vessels, even though those vessels posed limitations. With all of our varied emotions, needs, desires, we were unpredictable, yet necessary to the Phoenix's continued survival. We are interdependent. Each relying on the other to sustain our core, and to help protect the People from the ancient evils that constantly strive to unwork the weave of life."*

A sudden, violent wrenching sliced through Selena, and she gasped.

*Garethan.*

When Selena looked up, Anelees was fading before her, wisping away as if she were but smoke upon the wind.

"No!" Selena screamed, reaching for her.

*"You must decide, daughter."* Her voice blended with that of the Phoenix.

"But, I don't know how to control it yet!" Selena cried. "What if I destroy those I love while trying to annihilate Garethan!"

Another gut wrenching pull doubled Selena over.

*"Decide...before it is too late."*

## Chapter Seventeen

The hairs on the back of Serosen's neck stood on end. He glanced over at Eristta, and knew she felt it, too.

Dark and deadly magick was being wrought.

They increased their pace, sprinting like the wind up the tunnels and into the palace proper. The firewhits surged around them, a pulsating cloud of golden light.

*So close.*

The throne room loomed ahead, and Serosen could feel the palpable wave of dark power behind the closed doors. Peartoth, Culdhun, and several of the Drow mercenaries milled outside the door, terror and uncertainty on their faces.

When they noticed Serosen, Eristta and the firewhits approach, they dropped to their knees, Peartoth the first among them to bow his head, his entire body shaking.

"Sire," Peartoth and Culdhun said in unison.

"Stand," Serosen said.

They did, their faces pale and bewildered. "Ser, we don't understand what has happened," Peartoth said, his lips trembling. "One moment we were organizing our forces to search for your father, and the next thing we are here, and everyone is gone! We do not even know how these Drow came to be among us, and neither do they! What is happening?"

Serosen placed a calming hand upon his cousin's broad shoulder, feeling a measure of shame for doubting his loyalty. "Listen well. You have all been ensorcelled by Garethan's mages. The palace is empty. I do not know where our brothers-at-arms are, or whether they even live, but first we must carve out the canker that has lodged itself within our midst."

They turned as one to the throne room door. Magick, foul and tainted, leaked from around its seal, filling the hallway with a sickening green tint.

Eristta and a cloud of firewhits approached the door. "*He* is inside," they whispered as one, their many voices reverberating through the hall. Eristta looked at Serosen, her eyes flashing silver sparks. "And the mages are with him. As is Selena. And others…"

They sniffed the air. "Golems," Eristta choked out, their reek already penetrating into the hallway.

Serosen stepped forward, and without hesitation, Culdhun handed him his sword. The rest of the elves drew their weapons, the hiss of steel joining the droning beat of the firewhits wings.

"We fight not only for Whitecliff, brothers," Serosen said, including his attention to the Drow warriors that flanked him, their eyes dark and deadly, despite their fear. "But for *Tir na n-Og* itself. Know that Death Mages reside beyond this door, as well as the sorcerer and his filthy, unholy creations. Shield your eyes, and steel your hearts."

And with that, Serosen raised his hands, bespoke the ancient words of his people, drawing the energies of the land to him, before blasting the doors to singed bits with a mighty wave of elf-fire.

They swarmed inside. The force stopped and stared in awe at the scene at the foot of the dais steps. Garethan's entire form glowed, as a complicated spell writhed from his fingertips. A column of sickening crimson encircled Selena, winding around her limp body. Threads of orange spun away from the column and into the sorcerer's vibrating hands.

Serosen shouted his outrage, and rushed forward, sword in one hand, elf-fire erupting from the other. The firewhits joined his charge, their many voices raised in a deafening shriek as they arrowed toward the sorcerer's heart.

Only inches from their objective, Garethan turned his gaze to his attackers, and with a nod, flung them away like a broom swatting a fly.

Firewhits screeched in pain and fell from the air. Serosen flew and struck the dais steps with such force, he felt ribs crack and bones bruise.

*No! I must get to Selena!*

He forced himself to stand, only to come eye to hooded head with one of the Death Mages. The creature reached up to drop his cowl, and Serosen knew without a doubt, death arrived for him.

*"My heart, my soulmate,"* he elf-spoke to Selena, praying somehow she would hear his words. *"Forgive me for not being able to protect you. For not giving us the lifetime you so deserved to be loved, to be cherished.*

*"I love you,* mi'Awen, *now and forever."*

\* \* \* \* \*

*"I love you,* mi'Awen…*"*

Her soulmate's words lanced straight to her heart, and Selena ripped at the veil of pain that consumed her, fighting to the surface.

*"No! I'm coming, my dark prince! Don't leave me. Don't."*

Selena's eyes flew open. She looked past the grinning skull of Garethan, past the zipping, light-filled throngs of firewhits trying to distract the Death Mages who had opened virtual doorways that were belching filthy Golems, past her bond-sister and the force at her side that was hacking at the Golems, trying to drive them back.

Her gaze finally rested on her beloved, gripped in the power of one of the mages. His face was creased with pain, but even so, his thoughts were of her. Of her face. Her beautiful body. Of the times they had enjoyed the pleasure of each other's flesh. And he smiled grimly, resigned to his demise as the mage reached up to push his cowl away.

"NO!"

Selena's screech rocked the chamber, and all heads were forced in her direction, like moths to a flame. The entire room seemed to freeze in time. Golems stopped their ripping carnage. Death Mages dropped their hands and turned to face her. All of the elfin fighters' eyes riveted on the glowing personage within the writhing column of red.

Including Serosen.

Her dark prince.

"Selena!" he shouted. "Free yourself, *mi'Awen*! Do not let him win!"

*Choose...*

The Phoenix's voice flowed through her like liquid light, and Selena smiled, recognizing that she had made her choice the very moment she'd surrendered her heart and soul to the dark elf who had awakened her true essence.

Selena collapsed within herself, and with welcoming arms, flung open the door to her heart, unleashing the power that had burned dormant within her breast from that first breath of the Phoenix's ashes on the desolate roadway.

"No!" Garethan yelled, his eyes widening, his chest swelling with the abrupt backflow of the power he'd been attempting to absorb. "You shall not emerge! You shall not—"

The sorcerer was never able to finish his curse. The Phoenix emerged from the body that housed her, erupting in pure light from Selena's eyes and mouth...from the very heart of her being.

*And she was transformed.*

In Selena's stead winged a flaming, majestic creature. Its body shimmered and pulsed with blinding, multihued feathers, and with one small beat of her wings, Garethan's column shattered, fracturing off into dissipating shards of wild magick.

And she was free.

\* \* \* \* \*

The Phoenix rose above the stunned on-lookers, heat and power wafting off the ancient creature in stunning waves. The firewhits inclined their heads as one, their own heat pulsating brightly, like mini stars revolving around their gravitational sun.

"Goddess," Eristta whispered, dropping to her knees.

Serosen laughed, his heart rejoicing. *The Phoenix.* Of course.

His wife. His bride. A vessel of one of the ancients.

He laughed again, then turned to look grimly at the hooded horror that still held him in the grip of his power. "I would advise you to release me, mage."

The mage turned from the Phoenix to look once more upon the elf within its grasp. A rasping voice sawed across Serosen's flesh. *"She may yet slay me, but as it was before, she will be alone in this life, her heart bereft."*

Hands quick, the mage yanked his hood away, and Serosen closed his eyes, dread coursing through his body as the wild magick within the mage reached for him, pulling at his eyelids. Commanding his obedience.

*"Look at me, elf."*

*"Hold, my love!"* Selena's voice rang in his heart and Serosen gasped with the effort to resist. *"We come!"*

Scorching air coalesced around them, and before Serosen could draw breath, a fiery blast entered his body, leaving him untouched, yet crawling as if a living thing, down his arms and into the fingers of magick that tethered him to the mage.

The mage shrieked an inhuman, blood-curdling scream.

*Open your eyes...* came a voice, and this time Serosen recognized it as that of his powerful bride. He did just in time to see the Death Mage entirely disrobed, his skin marbled white and threaded with blue veins pulled tight over an emaciated frame. His hands were but claws, swiping stiffly at the Phoenix's magick that engulfed him. The great bird swooped down upon the evil spawn, golden beak open, flaming wings singeing the air before it.

Serosen stumbled backward into the arms of his sister.

The Phoenix sundered the magickal seams that held the mage's frail physical form together, and the demon burst apart in a shower of gore and noxious black smoke. The life essences it had stolen and absorbed, tumbled into the air, intoning their joy at being free of their captor, before melting away into the ether.

"What have you done?" came a booming shout.

All turned. Garethan had climbed the dais to stand beside the remaining Death Mage. He gripped the mage to keep from falling over, his body obviously weakened by Selena's shattering of his spell. But his eyes still writhed with hatred—and power. "This is not over." His gaze flicked from Serosen and Eristta to the Phoenix that hovered just above their heads. "You may be reborn, but I am not alone in my bid for power, shining one. Beware our wrath!"

The Phoenix screamed and streaked towards the sorcerer, but she was too late. The mage wove a quick, dark spell, and within a fraction of a second, they were gone, leaving naught but a tendril of smoke in their wake.

With the sudden absence of evil, the occupants of the room breathed a collective sigh of relief. The Golems that had been left behind fell into rotting piles of mud and sewage from which they were formed.

All eyes turned to the Phoenix, including those of Du'an who was just now waking from his convenient swoon. The great bird alighted upon the back of the crystal throne, its feathers undulating with brilliant magick as she tucked them to her sides. The firewhits bowed before her, and in moments everyone in the room did as well.

*"Rise,"* came the musical elf-speech of the ancient. *"None are to bow before me. I am not a Goddess, but a creature of the great spirit just as all of you are. And my current vessel would likely hound me for a millennia were I to allow worship."*

The Phoenix focused her fiery, amber gaze on Serosen. *"You have her heart, elf, and through your bonding you are both more than you were, as am I. We, all three, are linked in a trinity of power. The fire that burns in your veins lives also in hers and in turn, mine. Your power is great, even without us, but together we are a force to be reckoned with."*

Serosen felt the ancient's resigned sigh. *"And that power shall be needed. Pray others awaken and come to our aid, as I fear it will be beyond us to drive that foul demon back on our own."*

The great bird extended her energy and attention to the firewhits. *"My children. I am sorry, once again, for your sacrifice, but know that without your intervention, I would not have been reborn. My power would lie within the evil heart of Errabon, and all would be lost."*

A pain-wracked cough filled the chamber, and Eristta cried out and rushed to pluck Darous up off the floor. "Darous! Are you all right? I swear, you have more lives than a chimera!"

Laughter rumbled from the Phoenix, and she extended a tendril of power to stroke the frazzled Darous where he lay dazed upon Eristta's hand. Darous sighed in content, all vestiges of discomfort erased from his features. *"Yes. And he was so virtuous to not spill our secret until my vessel had accepted me. He is truly special."* The ribbon of energy brushed Eristta's cheek as the Phoenix pulled her power back. *"As are you."*

Eristta's face reddened, and Serosen laughed. He'd never seen his sibling blush. Usually she was making others flush crimson with her bold actions and words.

"By the Goddess," Du'an cried, then promptly fell back to the floor in an unconscious lump.

Ignoring the summer prince's dramatics, the Phoenix ruffled her feathers. Sparks danced up into the air, and she turned her gaze again to Serosen. *"It is time for me to take my leave. There is one who is clamoring to feel your arms, Princeling, and far be it for me to stand in her way."*

In the blink of an eye, the great bird shimmered and disappeared, leaving his beloved bride in its place. She stood on the seat of the throne, her body clothed in a rather transparent, multi-colored garment that hung loose about her shapely breasts and thighs like the plumage of a rare bird.

The silken feathers of a Phoenix.

Joy filled Selena's azure eyes as full awareness reasserted itself, and she leapt from the crystal throne with a cry and ran straight into Serosen's open arms.

## Chapter Eighteen

"Selena," said a cajoling voice. "You will be with him, soon, you have my word. We must prepare you properly for the ceremony."

Growling, Selena tugged at the miniscule, royal blue silken fabric that barely covered her finer assets. "Why do I have to wear *this*? What kind of ceremony has the guest of honor show up with her ass cheeks and nipples hanging out?"

Eristta smiled wickedly, then bit her lip. "Uh, a very complicated, secret Tuathan ceremony."

Selena *hmphed* and tried one more yank, then sighed and gave up. As she looked at her reflection in the mirror, she was comforted by the thought that at least she looked hot. Her near ankle-length tresses—which she now had to cut every morning—flowed seductively against her body, and her burgundy nipples peeked through the sheer fabric, the room's chill air making them pucker and ache for Serosen's lips. The thought of his mouth lapping at her breasts made Selena's pussy flood with moisture, and if her bond-sister had not been standing beside her, she would have plunged her fingers deep within the wetness and gone to town.

She'd been unable to think of anything for the past few hours but her dark prince whisking her away to a secluded spot where they could rut like out of control animals.

Eristta laughed, and Selena was quick to ward her thoughts. But she sighed and let her guard down once more. She had few secrets with Eristta, a sister at heart if not by blood.

"Truly, Selena, you will not be left wanting—long."

Selena gave Eristta a sideways glance, wondering at her words. She'd heard nothing from her for the past hour but how vital it was they perform this special ceremony to ensure her proper place among the Night Elves as their queen—even it was only temporary. It was imperative, according to those left of the Night Ranger guard, that a demesne not be rulerless, even for a short time among a world of very powerful, and in some cases, ambitious creatures.

After the scene in the throne room, she and Serosen hadn't had even an hour alone. There had been wounded to attend to. Wards to put into place. Spells and boundaries to erect once more, as well as warnings to send out to the other Kingdomes. And then there was the small matter of locating the entirety of Whitecliff's Rangers, retainers, and most importantly, their father and their brother Vigil. They suffered a second terrible blow when they learned that the sanctuary where the Night Elfin women hid had been desecrated, and all of the women and children—taken.

The memory of her lover's and his sister's deep anguish when they'd heard the news pierced her soul, and Selena had been hard-pressed to contain the terrible need to call upon the Phoenix and go after the bastards that had taken them. But she knew it was vital to be very, very select in the moments in which she unleashed the Ancient One.

If Eristta had remained at the sanctuary, she too, would have been taken.

Selena drew in a calming breath and smiled at her beautiful and exotic bond-sister. Everything in its time and place. There was much preparation needed before they could face Garethan again, which was what her soulmate had been attending to the past twenty-four hours. First, they *must* locate their fighting force. Selena sensed that they were very much alive—but was unable to establish where.

A cool hand rested on her bare shoulder. "Sister. Do not worry so. We will find them. We will rebuild, and gather an army great enough to fight the evil that has despoiled the land." Eristta took her hand and led her out of the room. "Come. It is time."

They traversed the grand halls, to arrive at a section of the palace Selena did not recognize. Which was no surprise. Whitecliff was immense, and Selena knew it would be months before she could find her way around.

As they passed the carvings of ancient beasts and mysterious symbols, Selena thought of her friend Gwen, and a pang of homesickness filled her. Not that she wanted to return to her old life, but she would miss Gwen terribly. Her gentle, angelic nature was like a balm to Selena's fiery soul, and the thought of never seeing her again left her melancholy.

They walked up to another intricately carved lintel, and Selena paused to stare wide-eyed, thoughts of her friend taking a back seat. The carving sported naked, cavorting nymphs of every size and hue, pleasuring themselves, and one another, their fey faces frozen in rapturous expressions and winsome, intimate smiles.

Desire curled in Selena's belly, and she licked dry lips. "Well, that's something," she murmured. Eristta giggled beside her, then shoved her under the lintel and into the room.

Selena sucked in a startled breath as she passed through what she knew by now to be a magickal barrier. On the other side, she found herself standing in a room of foggy swirls and soft blue sky. The ground under her feet was as supple as new summer grass, and the air a pleasant, intoxicating temperature.

"What's this?" Selena asked, as she walked further in.

*The pleasure room.*

The memory burst into her thoughts, and Selena smiled, realizing it was just another vestige of her lover's knowledge.

A large, oblong divan covered in pale pink rose petals and luxurious elfin satin sat in the center of the room. The bed beckoned her, and intrigued, Selena walked over and sat. She closed her eyes and delved her fingers into the silky material, the heady scent of roses and nicotiana filling her senses.

Selena felt her head lighten, as if she'd just downed a double-shot shot of tequila. A languid warmth spread through her belly, and her thoughts seemed at once sharper and misty, all at the same time.

A warm breeze teased her nearly bare body, and a giggle followed. Selena opened her eyes to stare into the clear jade gaze of one of the most beautiful creatures she had ever seen. "Who are you?" Selena asked breathlessly.

The lithe, perfectly formed fey woman leaned in, her smile warm. Honeyed locks flowed down her back and rested against her pert, pale breasts. "I am whoever you want me to be," the woman replied softly.

"As am I."

Selena turned her head to see another fey woman. This one dark of skin, with crystal clear blue eyes, and an exceptionally full bosom. Her pointed, jewel tipped nipples stood out bright red against smooth, dusky skin. She glided closer, her short-cropped copper hair glistening. She sat on the divan next to Selena and reached out a delicate hand.

"We are here to please you, my Queen," said the darker elf. "You may call me Carien." She motioned to her fair cousin. "And she is Tarras."

Selena sucked in a startled breath as Carien's fingers drew a delicate trail down her neck to the swell of her breasts beneath the sheer fabric. The pale elf leaned in closer. With a sly smile, Tarras dipped her head and flicked a pink tongue across Selena's puckered nipple.

Selena gasped, wholly unprepared for such contact. But her mind was foggy, and the forbidden sensation shot straight through to her pussy, which responded instantly, dampening the short curls. A quick image of Serosen between her legs, teasing at her aching clit sent pulses of wild desire coursing through her.

"Serosen! What type of ceremony is this!" she yelled, struggling against the dizziness.

Tarras placed a warm hand on Selena's arm. "Peace, my Queen. You have nothing to fear from our attentions. Nor are you being unfaithful by enjoying our ministrations, for you see..." Both elves stood, their stunning bodies mirroring each other, dark to light. "We are but a creation of Serosen's imagination...and your own," they finished in synch.

And Selena did see. *They are not real.* Not flesh and blood, but rather artful illusions borne of her own carnal imaginings. Selena laughed, her body flushing. Even so, their touches felt real. Their hands...the pale one's tongue...

*"Relax. Enjoy,* mi'Awen. *Let them prepare you for my touch. For my tongue. For my swollen cock."*

"Serosen!" Selena elf-spoke, searching for her lover's presence.

He gently pushed her spirit fingers aside with a chuckle. *"I would watch your pleasure, Selena. See your passionate need, hear your cries of rapture. Do you deny me this?"*

Selena felt his deep love, his wanting to bring her a pleasure she had yet to experience, holding back his own passionate need.

She smiled wantonly and drew herself up. "Oh, you want to watch, eh?" Selena looked at Tarras and Carien, their eyes focused hungrily on her, their lips slightly parted. A tiny thrill of fear and a greater one of expectancy surged through her. "Come," she whispered to the two women. "Do with me as you will."

Slowly, they approached. The dark one behind her, the fairer one kneeling in front of her. Carien kneaded her shoulders, her touch light yet penetrating, forcing her to relax.

"You are beautiful," Tarras murmured as she drew her hands along the inside of Selena's thighs, moving them slightly apart. The blue fabric inched up, exposing all of Selena's intimate flesh to Tarras's eyes.

Selena sucked in breath as the pale elf's hand brushed her mound, then a single finger slipped between her hot folds.

A groan eased from her throat, and Selena threw back her spinning head. With gentle hands Tarras eased her legs further apart, while at the same time, Carien's hands moved down from her shoulders to cup her heavy, throbbing breasts.

"So perfect," Carien whispered, her breath minty cool as it blew across Selena's ear.

*"Oh, sweet torture!"* Selena gasped in elf-speak, her desire viciously heightened by the thought of Serosen watching their wanton display.

Just as she was about to demand Serosen's presence, a warm tongue darted against her clit, and Selena bucked against the elf's perfect face. Quick to sense her mistress's near climax, Carien pinched Selena's taut nipples, rolling them between her delicate fingers while Tarras grinned wickedly and dipped her head in for another taste, this time sucking on Selena's sensitive clit.

Selena's body jerked with her orgasm, and she sensed Serosen's pulsating response to her release. Felt his smoky eyes on her as she lay exposed to the ministration of the two ethereal creatures.

As the liquid sensations ebbed, Selena raised her head. The mists parted to reveal her dark prince. Naked, his muscled perfection rippled with each stride toward the bed. His cock stood rigid, like a weather vane pointing in the direction of a wild storm.

"Serosen," Selena whispered, her body vibrating with longing and deep hunger.

As he thundered up to the divan, Tarras and Carien dissolved into the ether, their pleased smiles lingering in Selena's mind.

Until her lover reached her. "You are truly wicked, *mi'Awen*, to tease me so." His hot hands found her. They gripped the firm roundness of her ass, and before she could respond, her dark prince knelt and delved into her dripping box where Tarras had tasted her nectar. But Serosen's demanding tongue gave her no quarter. Selena gripped his dark head as another wave of orgasm took hold.

She screamed, the powerful sensations making her blood pound fast and hot. "Ohmygod, here we go again," Selena whispered.

Serosen left her honeyed core, and drew his taut body even with hers, his eyes capturing her full attention. "Must we involve the Gods?" Serosen asked, and Selena realized in shock that he was serious.

She couldn't help her smile, before reaching out to stroke his strong, chiseled jaw. Leaning in, Selena touched her lips to his, relishing her own sweet nectar upon his tongue. She licked the side of his mouth, feeling a wild need to have him deep inside her.

"No Gods or Goddesses, then," Selena murmured. "Unless they are here to bless our union."

With a guttural growl, Serosen bore her back onto the bed, his mouth capturing hers in a bruising kiss that thrilled Selena straight to her throbbing center.

He drew her hands above her head, exposing her scantily clad breasts. With his other hand he ripped the material from her body and flung it away, his eyes raking her curves with animal need.

"How I have longed to feel myself buried within your tight quim," Serosen said, his voice hoarse with desire. "To feel you writhe beneath me. To hear your lustful cries, and know that none of this has simply been a dream."

Selena started at his words, as he gave voice to her own fears. She reached up and encircled his powerful neck with her arms, pressing her breasts to his sculpted chest. "It was not a dream, my love. We are together." Selena kissed the pulse that throbbed at the base of his throat. "Forever, my dark prince."

Moaning, her lover reached beneath her upper thighs with both arms, before plunging his thick rod into her slick pussy.

*Lord have mercy*, Selena thought, as raw pleasure shot straight to her head, leaving her dizzy and disoriented. Stroke, after powerful stroke, Serosen plunged within her channel, Selena meeting each of his thrusts, her knees nearly touching her shoulders to allow him deeper penetration.

Minutes flew, her dark lover's rhythm never slowing, never breaking as he spoke words of love in his native tongue. Selena gasped with pure, unbridled delight, her pussy contracting again and again around the fullness of her lover's cock.

As before, Selena felt the combined sensations of their *danu awen* build. But this time, there was more. *They* were more. Her inner fire burned bright, heightening the vibrations and soul-shattering connection she felt with her soulmate. And Serosen's own true nature answered her call, blending, merging with her spirit as they both neared climax.

In that instant, the combined force of their merging *danu awen* uplifted their very souls, flinging them free of their earthly bodies into the world between worlds.

Floating in the pleasant, neutral world of mist and light, the two lovers clung to one another, their desires sated—for a moment. Peace, and a deep sense of promise filled their hearts.

"Does this normally happen?" Selena asked.

Serosen chuckled softly. "No. We seem to break new ground, wife, wherever we go."

Selena sighed in contentment, and wrapped her spirit arms around her husband, feeling that perhaps their future *could* be filled with beauty and happiness and life.

As long as they were together.

Suddenly the veil parted, and out walked a great warrior, his face painted with the symbols of life, his heavily muscled body shining even in the unobtrusive light of the ether world.

He stopped before the couple, and inclined his head. "My brother, sister. Forgive the intrusion. I was unable to come to you in my physical form, but seeing an opportunity to do so in spirit, I took it."

Selena gave a small cry of joy, and Serosen stepped forward to clasp the spirit hand of his hunt brother. "Red Claw! I feared for your safety, and am overjoyed to see you, if only in spirit." Serosen raised his brow. "You are not…you have not…"

"Passed?" Red Claw finished for him with a smile. He shook his head. "No. My physical body still pulses with the blood of my forefathers deep in a secluded glade where even now, I wait out my pursuers." Red Claw brushed hair away from his face. "They will not find me, of course, but I cannot bear to sit idle. There is much to do, my brother, in preparing for what is to come."

Serosen nodded, all three standing silent for a moment, remembering, and dreading the battle ahead.

Red Claw turned to Selena. He studied her with a keen eye, and Selena straightened. Damned if she'd be found wanting by this graceful, awesome human being. "Sister, I sensed your acceptance of power, and in that moment, recognized your true self from my camp so many leagues away." He smiled down on her, and Selena found herself propelled into his secure arms.

"Did you know, Red Claw, what I was that day in the glade?"

He released her and exchanged a look with his elfin brother. "No. I knew you were other than you seemed, but I didn't understand what resided at your heart." Red Claw brushed a large hand down the side of her head. "You are blessed, sister, and yet also charged with a grave responsibility. I know you will bear it well."

His words meant so much to her, Selena could scarce reply.

"There is something I must ask you," Red Claw began, and Selena looked on in shock as Serosen surged between them with a growl.

"Leave off, brother. You do not need to do this."

Red Claw stepped around Serosen, his expression grave. "I beg your forgiveness, brother, but you know it must be done."

Confusion rushed through Selena, and she reached for her dark prince's hand, drawing him to her side. "What's going on?"

Moving to stand directly before her, Red Claw looked down with patient, dark eyes. "I have to ask you, Selena, what is your greatest desire?"

He spoke the words softly, but Selena heard them as they had been given life within her very breast. Without hesitation she turned to her dark prince and captured his gray eyes with her own penetrating gaze. "To remain at my soulmate's side. Now and unto forever. Even in death will I stand beside him."

A palpable sense of relief coursed through the air, and Selena narrowed her gaze at Red Claw. "Why would you ask a question like that?"

Red Claw smiled warmly, and looked at his hunt brother. "Can I say I told you so?"

Serosen *hmphed* in response and crossed his arms, but a grin tugged at his lips.

*"Mother…Father…I am coming…"*

"Did you hear that?" Selena asked, her head whipping to stare into the mists that swirled about them.

Serosen cocked his head. "A voice…"

Red Claw laughed, and with a subtle nod of his head, reverted to his totem shape. The great bear, rust red in color this time, lumbered into the mist and disappeared from view.

A quickening in Selena's abdomen brought her crashing back into her physical body where it lay entwined with her lover's upon the divan. Serosen rose onto his elbows, a hesitant joy filling his smoky gaze, and Selena shot into an upright position, her heart racing.

"You don't think…"

Her dark prince pressed a large, warm hand to her abdomen, his grin wide. "What I think doesn't matter. I imagine our offspring will have a will and mind all of its own."

"Oh, *Tia* Sophia," Selena said, her heart near to bursting as Selena's hand covered that of her husband. "I think you may have a grandniece or nephew beginning its journey into the world."

# Epilogue
## The Forest of EverNight
## on the Border of Whitecliff Demesne

Eristta notched her bow, and pressed herself tight against the glowing florescent lichen that coated the boulders at Ethlinn.

"Damn, but these creatures are impossible to track," she whispered to no one in particular. None of the stoic Drow ever seemed to feel the need to communicate at all, let alone respond to such an obvious statement.

The dark elf sighed and lowered her bow. She'd accompanied the Drow back to their homeland to warn them of the sorcerer's treachery, and to try and convince them to reunite their forces with that of the Winter Kingdome.

But it hadn't gone quite as Eristta had planned. The Drow leader turned out to be a nefarious, slippery sort of indeterminate temperament, and instead of pledging his loyalty and support, challenged Eristta with a mission, destroy the Carrion bird that had been decimating the prey in the EverNight forest, and he would *consider* her offer.

Eristta's lip curled. *Consider it.* Who did he think he was? She didn't have time for this nonsense. She had a brother and father to find. An army to gather.

And not for the first time, Eristta thought how much easier everything would be, if that damned elusive Red

Claw were around to assist. Where in Balor's Realm was he? If he was so all-knowing as Serosen believed him to be, why hadn't he been there to protect the women and children in their sanctuary? Or to prevent the taking of Whitecliff?

A bright flare of loss filled Eristta, and she closed her eyes.

"It comes," whispered the Drow warrior behind her.

Eristta's violet eyes snapped open, and she stilled her thoughts, her intent focused on the forest around her. *There.* Just beyond the jagged rocks that speared the glade to her right. A shimmer in the natural calm. Something dark. Something big.

As Eristta murmured her personal words of power. Energy surged along the oghms and vines that wound each wrist and up on either side of her breasts. Silver glints flashed within her eyes as she mind-reached to her prey.

The fine thread of her *danu awen* collided with the primitive, hateful energy of her prey, and Eristta mentally reared back with a gasp. Eristta heard a snicker behind her as she withdrew her tendrils of magick.

Her lip curled, but she wasted no time on the smug Drow warrior. *Time to end this.* Incanting a protection spell, Eristta surged towards the disturbance, arrows at the ready. Twenty yards. Ten. She still couldn't see the bird. Consummate "blenders," Carrion birds adapted their coloring to their environment.

But she could feel it. Sense its dark, pulsating heart.

Kneeling, Eristta let loose a quick bevy of arrows. She guided them true, and smiled in grim satisfaction as each thunked solidly into their mark.

A terrible shriek fractured the night, and without pause, Eristta dropped her bow, drew her kriss and advanced. She'd cut out the beast's still beating heart and deliver that to the Drow commander.

Ten feet. Four. Eristta realized her error only inches from her prey. A noxious blast of fetid air hit her face, and she nearly choked.

*By the Goddess.*

It wasn't simply one Carrion bird. It was a mother and her four hatchlings. Too late to stop, Eristta dived and rolled between the furious mother bird's massive-clawed talons, and past the wicked spearing beaks of the four man-sized younglings.

*Think, Eristta. Think!*

She came out of her roll behind the enraged and hungry troop, and crouched, facing them. Eristta knew she could kill the younger birds one by one, but not with their mother intent on gutting her. And besides, nuisance or not, it didn't set well with her to wipe out an entire family of any creature, save those of demon design.

And these were fey creatures, if obnoxious ones. Now, if they had attacked her, it would be different. But here, she was the huntress.

The mother bird flapped her enormous, land-bound wings and urged her hatchlings forward with a soul piercing cry.

*Ah, yes,* thought Eristta as she swallowed her fear. *The good mother is using this opportunity to teach her offspring to hunt.*

Me.

## About the author:

Nelissa welcomes mail from readers. You can write to her c/o Ellora's Cave Publishing at 1056 Home Avenue, Akron OH 44310-3502.

# Why an electronic book?

We live in the Information Age—an exciting time in the history of human civilization in which technology rules supreme and continues to progress in leaps and bounds every minute of every hour of every day. For a multitude of reasons, more and more avid literary fans are opting to purchase e-books instead of paperbacks. The question to those not yet initiated to the world of electronic reading is simply: *why?*

1. *Price.* An electronic title at Ellora's Cave Publishing and Cerridwen Press runs anywhere from 40-75% less than the cover price of the exact same title in paperback format. Why? Cold mathematics. It is less expensive to publish an e-book than it is to publish a paperback, so the savings are passed along to the consumer.
2. *Space.* Running out of room to house your paperback books? That is one worry you will never have with electronic novels. For a low one-time cost, you can purchase a handheld computer designed specifically for e-reading purposes. Many e-readers are larger than the average handheld, giving you plenty of screen room. Better yet, hundreds of titles can be stored within your new library—a single microchip. (Please note that Ellora's Cave and Cerridwen Press does not endorse any specific brands. You can check our website at www.ellorascave.com or

www.cerridwenpress.com for customer recommendations we make available to new consumers.)
3. *Mobility.* Because your new library now consists of only a microchip, your entire cache of books can be taken with you wherever you go.
4. *Personal preferences are accounted for.* Are the words you are currently reading too small? Too large? Too...**ANNOYING**? Paperback books cannot be modified according to personal preferences, but e-books can.
5. *Instant gratification.* Is it the middle of the night and all the bookstores are closed? Are you tired of waiting days—sometimes weeks—for online and offline bookstores to ship the novels you bought? Ellora's Cave Publishing sells instantaneous downloads 24 hours a day, 7 days a week, 365 days a year. Our e-book delivery system is 100% automated, meaning your order is filled as soon as you pay for it.

Those are a few of the top reasons why electronic novels are displacing paperbacks for many an avid reader. As always, Ellora's Cave and Cerridwen Press welcomes your questions and comments. We invite you to email us at service@ellorascave.com, service@cerridwenpress.com or write to us directly at: 1056 Home Ave. Akron OH 44310-3502.

NEED A MORE EXCITING
WAY TO PLAN YOUR DAY?

# ELLORA'S
# CAVEMEN
2006 CALENDAR

COMING THIS FALL

# The ELLORA'S CAVE Library

Stay up to date with Ellora's Cave Titles in Print with our Quarterly Catalog.

To recieve a catalog,
send an email with your name
and mailing address to:

CATALOG@ELLORASCAVE.COM

or send a letter or postcard
with your mailing address to:
Catalog Request
c/o Ellora's Cave Publishing, Inc.
1337 Commerce Drive #13
Stow, OH 44224

Discover for yourself why readers can't get enough of the multiple award-winning publisher Ellora's Cave. Whether you prefer e-books or paperbacks, be sure to visit EC on the web at www.ellorascave.com for an erotic reading experience that will leave you breathless.

www.ellorascave.com